There was a part of Sydney that still wanted to trust Connors. What if her instincts were wrong? What if Connors had no idea who Christopher and May were and Sydney was leaving him in jeopardy if she fled? Her father's voice scolded her and began rattling off a laundry list of people that she had mistakenly trusted in the past. *Sloane, your mother* . . . She shook her head to shut him up. "You're not helping right now," she whispered, briefly wondering if talking out loud to the voices in her head was enough to earn her a permanent spot at the Devereaux.

Obviously, the right thing to do was get out, call for help, and wait for the APO team to arrive. Just the thought of leaving the clinic made her father's voice downgrade from "warning" to "approval" level in her mind. There was absolutely no doubt about it: Getting out now was the safest course of action. Sydney stood up, took a deep breath, and—not for the first time in her life—decided to ignore the safest course of action.

ALIAS™

THE
APO™
SERIES

THE GHOST

BY BRIAN STUDLER

An original novel based on the
hit TV series created by J. J. Abrams

SSE
SIMON SPOTLIGHT ENTERTAINMENT
New York London Toronto Sydney

SSE

SIMON SPOTLIGHT ENTERTAINMENT
An imprint of Simon & Schuster
1230 Avenue of the Americas, New York, New York 10020

Manufactured in the United States of America
First Edition 10 9 8 7 6 5 4 3 2 1
Library of Congress Control Number 2006925829
ISBN-13: 978-1-4169-2444-9
ISBN-10: 1-4169-2444-2

The author wishes to dedicate this book to his mother, the ALIAS fan.

ALIAS™

CHAPTER 1

SANTA MONICA FARMER'S MARKET

"Two bucks. Best price on heirloom tomatoes in the whole United States," the man in the blue overalls announced. Sydney Bristow smiled at him and switched her large, canvas shopping bag from her left shoulder to her right.

"Sorry. I already picked up tomatoes around the corner," she said. *And they were cheaper,* Sydney thought, looking over the man's display of vegetables.

It was an exceptionally beautiful morning in Los Angeles, and Sydney was making the most of it. *I love the farmer's market,* she thought as she walked down the street, perusing the produce and flower stalls. *It's a nice change of pace,* she thought, eyeing some particularly fine-looking asparagus. *No one shooting at me, no bombs to disarm . . . I'd much rather decide between red and yellow bell peppers than between cutting the red or yellow wire on a ten-megaton nuke—like I had to yesterday.*

On a whim, Sydney opted to buy the red *and* yellow peppers. As she handed her money to the older Chinese woman at the stall, the hairs on the back of Syd's neck tingled. *Something's not right,* she thought. Knowing better than to dismiss a warning signal, no matter how small, Sydney quickly took stock of the situation. Smiling, being careful not to seem alarmed, she scanned the market. Nothing seemed out of the ordinary . . . until she caught the quick flash of sunlight off a camera lens. Sydney adjusted her position so that she could see the photographer reflected in the rear view mirror of the seller's van. There he was: a middle-aged man with an expensive digital camera, lurking behind a display of organic honey and definitely taking pictures of Syd. He didn't look threatening, but Sydney had learned to never gauge an opponent based solely on appearance.

"I think you have an admirer," the Chinese woman said, handing Sydney her change.

Sydney laughed. *Okay,* Syd thought. *Even the bell pepper lady spotted this guy. This is not professional surveillance.* Thanking the woman, Sydney moved down the street, one eye on the man with the camera.

As Sydney came to the intersection of Second and Arizona, the center of the market, she caught a glimpse of the man reflected in a mylar balloon tied to the bumper of a pickup truck full of strawberries. He was closer than before. She could even hear the sound of the camera's shutter. *Getting a little cocky, aren't you,* Syd thought. *Time to find out who you are.*

Sydney turned down Arizona, noting with satisfaction that the increasingly bold photographer followed after her. Hoping to maneuver him toward the far end of the market, she lingered over a display of cheap, designer-knockoff sunglasses. Once she saw the man pass by her in the mirrored lens of a pair of "Pradoo" glasses, Sydney turned and walked rapidly toward him. Spooked, the photographer spun around and started making his way toward the far end of the street. *Perfect . . . exactly what I wanted you to do.*

Syd was closing the gap, drawing within a few feet of the fast-walking stranger, when her shopping bag was grabbed from her hand. *Damn,* she thought, *why now?* The thief, a clean-cut kid in his early twenties, was racing away from her . . . back toward the center of the market. If it were only a question of stolen produce, she might let it go, but her keys and her cell phone were in that bag as well. With a regretful last glance at the vanishing photographer, Sydney turned and took off after the purse snatcher.

The market was crowded, but the thief was making good time. Sydney ran as fast as she could, trying hard not to plow anyone over. "Stop him!" Sydney shouted, hoping that someone would at least try to slow the guy down. "He's got my bag!"

The crowd was thinning as Sydney neared the end of the market, but the thief was almost completely in the clear. *As soon as he rounds that corner, he's going to be a lot harder to catch.* With a final burst of speed, Sydney cut left and cleanly vaulted a table of beautiful watermelon slices. Two strides later she caught up to the thief and swept his legs from under him with a well-placed kick.

He went down hard, dropping Sydney's bag in an attempt to shield his face from the onrushing asphalt. As he lay there, gasping for breath, Syd spun around and, kneeling on the man's back, twisted one of his arms behind his back.

A smattering of applause and laughter drew Sydney's attention: quite a little crowd had gathered. *Great,* she thought. *Undercover agents are not exactly encouraged to make scenes in public.* Afraid that any moment now a policeman would show up, Sydney turned her attention back to the thief. "This could be your lucky day. I don't feel like filling out a police report," she said. Syd got off of the man's back, allowing him to get to his feet. As he wiped the gravel off of his skinned knees and elbows, Sydney got her first good look at the guy. *This isn't a purse snatcher,* she thought. *This is a frat boy.*

The guy looked at her sheepishly, then spoke. "Look, I'm sorry. Some guy said he'd pay me five hundred bucks if I could grab your purse and make it to the far end of the street. I thought it was just some reality TV thing."

"Five hundred . . . what guy? Point him out to me," Sydney demanded.

The would-be thief looked around at the crowd. Many of the onlookers were openly laughing at him. He shook his head. "I don't see him. He was just some weird old dude. Had on a fancy suit with a white rose in the . . . ummm . . ."

"Lapel?" Syd offered.

"Yeah. The lapel. But he ain't here now."

Sydney was confused but decided to extricate herself from the situation altogether. She'd already drawn too much attention. "Okay, get out of here. And don't go grabbing anyone else's bag . . . no matter how much someone offers you."

The frat guy smiled gratefully. "I'm sorry," he said. Syd just nodded and waved him off. He turned to leave, stopped, and turned back. "Hey, do you have a boyfriend?" he called to Sydney.

Sydney did her best to suppress a laugh. "You have got to be kidding me." The guy just shrugged a *can't blame a guy for trying* shrug and walked away.

As she picked up her bag from the ground, Sydney heard the familiar click of a camera shutter. Looking up, she saw the photographer standing at the edge of the crowd . . . snapping off one shot after another. Sydney was fed up with the course that her morning was taking. *What happened to my day off?* She rushed the shutterbug. Before he could react, she had grabbed the man's camera and, with impressive speed, put him in a chokehold by twisting the strap around his neck, while simultaneously thumbing open the camera's side door and ejecting the memory card.

"Why are you taking pictures of me? Talk," Sydney said, giving the camera strap a sharp tug for emphasis.

"Please, Miss Bristow. You're hurting me."

How does this guy know my name? Sydney wondered.

The crowd was gathering again, some of them starting to wonder out loud if Sydney was some kind of lunatic, and the photographer looked genuinely terrified. "I'm sorry, Ms. Bristow. He said he was your colleague. He told me it was just a practical joke he was playing on you."

Sydney released the pressure on the camera strap. "Who did? Where is he?" She asked.

The man glanced around the crowd, then back

to Sydney. "He's not here. The man in the suit. He gave me five hundred dollars to follow you and take your picture. Please don't hurt me."

This has gone far enough.

Loudly, for the benefit of the crowd, she feigned a fit of embarrassed laughter. "Oh my God. This must be one of Steve's jokes. I didn't hurt you, did I?" Sydney helped the man untangle himself from his camera strap, apologizing profusely the entire time. *Time to beat a hasty retreat.*

Sydney walked away from the market as fast as she could go without drawing any more attention to herself. Just as she was rounding the corner onto Ocean Avenue, her phone started to ring. Fishing it from the depths of her bag, Sydney noted that the call was from her partner, Marcus Dixon. "Hey, Dixon, what's up?"

"Don't shoot the messenger," he replied. "I hate to do it to you on your day off, Syd, but Sloane's called a briefing for two o'clock. Looks like we have a new assignment." *Great.*

As she hung up the phone, Sydney felt someone tugging at the hem of her shirt. She spun around, ready to fight it out, only to find an eight-year-old girl holding a white rose. Sydney dropped her hands from their attack position as the little girl held out the flower.

"The man gave me money and said to give you this. He said he would see you at the office," she said with a shy smile, and then walked away.

CHAPTER 2

LOS ANGELES

The train rattled along beneath the streets of downtown Los Angeles, carrying the late-morning crowd to their destinations. Alone on a bench at the back of the very last car, Sydney Bristow contemplated the white rose, now sealed in a ziptop bag. It gave every appearance of being a normal flower, but Sydney intended to have Marshall check it out just the same. Better safe than sorry.

The metallic screech of brakes drew Sydney's attention as the train pulled to a stop. The doors hissed open and a handful of people moved to exit the car. Syd gathered her belongings, stuffing the rose back into her purse, and slipped off the train just before the doors slid shut again.

Sydney glanced around, making sure that she was unobserved, and then made her way toward the end of the platform. She passed a man in a transit authority uniform sweeping the already spotless floor. As she moved past him, he made eye contact and gave an almost imperceptible nod: all clear to enter.

She slipped around the edge of the platform, past a barricade, and entered a door marked AUTHORIZED PERSONNEL ONLY. Once inside, she flipped a series of breakers and switches, disengaging the massive locks on the blast-proof doors of APO headquarters.

The gleaming white hallways of APO were busier than usual. Junior agents dashed from office to office, gathering information from their senior counterparts and distributing it as needed. Sydney pulled the plastic bag containing the rose from her purse and turned down a back corridor, headed for Marshall's workshop.

As Syd approached his door, APO's resident tech wizard, Marshall J. Flinkman, burst out of his office carrying a steaming mug of coffee. Attempting to move as quickly as possible without spilling any of the scalding liquid on his own hand, Marshall pushed past Sydney without acknowledging her presence.

"Marshall . . . ," Sydney called after him, holding up the bag. "Could you . . . ?"

Marshall glanced up from the mug, just long enough to see the rose in Sydney's hand, and then let out an agonized wail as he disappeared around the corner: "White roses. Why didn't I think of that? Everyone knows he loves white roses."

"What is going on around here?" Sydney muttered as she followed Marshall's trail of coffee splashes around the corner, which led straight across the floor of the bull pen and into the glassed-in briefing room that occupied the center of the cavernous space. Through the glass, Sydney could see her fellow agents gathered around the conference table. There was Michael Vaughn, her boyfriend—just the sight of him made Sydney smile—sitting next to his lifelong friend Eric Weiss. Marcus Dixon, her partner ever since her first days in intelligence, was also present. At the head of the table, standing with his back to the wall of high-tech video monitors, was Arvin Sloane, the head of APO and the most evil man that Sydney had ever had the displeasure of knowing. The focus of all their attention was sitting at the conference table—a dapper gentleman in an expensive-looking, blue and white seersucker suit.

As the stranger accepted the cup that Marshall reverentially offered to him, Sydney noticed the immaculate white rose in the lapel of his suit. She watched in amazement as the man took a sip of the coffee and then, apparently finding the brew to his liking, reached out and patted Marshall on the head like a puppy.

A familiar voice came from behind Sydney. "If Marshall had a tail, he'd be wagging it." Sydney turned to find that her half sister, Nadia Santos, had joined her. Nadia was Sloane's daughter—the product of an affair with Sydney's mother—but, in spite of their twisted family history, Sydney had grown to love and trust her sister completely.

"Nadia, who is that? Marshall looks like he's going to faint." Sydney took note of the rapt attention that Sloane and her fellow agents were paying to the stranger. "Actually, they all look like they're going to faint."

"I don't know. They've been like this for the last two hours, ever since that man arrived. I wanted to go meet him, see what all the fuss was about, but I'm trying to finish up the report on the Madagascar mission. We're delaying the start of the briefing until your father gets here."

"Does our visitor have a name?" Sydney inquired.

Nadia shrugged. "Not as far as I know. Marshall said something about the 'Ghost' being here, but he was a little too excited to pass along anything as helpful as a name."

Sydney looked back toward the briefing room, her face taking on the same fascinated expression that Vaughn and the others shared. "The Ghost? You're kidding me. I always assumed that he was just a rumor. Like the boogeyman for young agents. No wonder Marshall's excited. The Ghost is an obsession of his."

Now it was Nadia's turn to be curious. "Who is the Ghost? How come I've never heard of him?"

"Not that many people remember him, I guess. His heyday was some time in the seventies. Like I said, I wasn't even sure that he ever really existed."

"What do you know about him?"

Sydney continued to stare at their visitor as she answered. "He's a legend. If even half of what they say about him were true, he'd be the greatest psy-ops genius of all time. Supposedly he is so far underground and has changed aliases so many times that no one knows his true identity anymore. Some people say that even *he* doesn't remember who he is."

Nadia laughed. "That's not genius. That's delusional. And if that were the case, how do we know that the man in there"—Nadia pointed to the briefing room—"is really who he says he is."

Sydney shook her head, finally tearing her eyes away from the man in the suit and turning to face her sister. "I don't know. The only thing we know for certain is that if he got clearance to enter this facility, he must have some very highly placed connections." Sydney held up the plastic bag for Nadia to see. "And we know that he likes white roses."

"Where did you get that?"

"It was given to me at the farmer's market this morning. A gift from the Ghost, apparently."

Nadia looked confused. "Have you two already met?"

"No. Not face-to-face, at any rate. But I think that it's time I introduced myself." Sydney excused herself from Nadia and headed for the briefing room, ready to meet a ghost.

CHAPTER 3

APO HEADQUARTERS

As Sydney entered the briefing room, the well-dressed man was holding forth on the history of the MK-ULTRA project. Upon seeing Sydney, he cut himself off in mid-sentence and practically jumped to his feet.

Sloane smiled at her . . . that reptilian smile that never failed to make Sydney's blood run cold. Crossing the room toward Sydney, Sloane attempted to make an introduction. "And this is Ms.—"

The stranger spoke up before Sloane could

finish. "Ms. Bristow. Yes. What a pleasure. Truly, Ms. Bristow, a very great pleasure indeed. I have been following your remarkable career ever since its inception and may I just say that the very thought of working with you thrills me to the core. Please forgive me my little stunt at the market this morning, but I really could not resist the opportunity to observe you in action, so to speak. And, as expected, you did not disappoint. Bravo, Ms. Bristow. Very well played; very well played, indeed. Ah . . . but I can see that you are a little confused by all of this. Please don't fret, my dear. . . . All will be made clear in time. For now, just know that you can call me Mr. Connors, and that I am overjoyed to finally make the acquaintance of the daughter of the finest man with whom I ever had the privilege to serve."

Completely flustered by the torrent of words that Mr. Connors had unleashed, all that Sydney could manage was a feeble "Um . . ."

While Sloane and her fellow agents expressed their curiosity about the "stunt at the market," Sydney took a better look at the strange man smiling at her from across the room. He was slightly shorter than average, but gave the impression of being powerfully built underneath his impeccably tailored suit. He appeared to be in his mid-sixties, but the youthful sparkle of his eyes and his wide, apparently genuine smile gave a definite impression of youth and vitality. His voice was slightly high-pitched and he spoke rapidly, with no discernible accent. Sydney suspected that the man's convoluted speech patterns and curiously flattened accent were designed to conceal any information about his origins. On the table next to him were a battered leather briefcase and an umbrella. *Quite the dandy,* she thought.

Connors's expectant smile and unwavering gaze snapped Sydney out of her reverie. She crossed the room and shook the man's outstretched hand. "I'm sorry. You really threw me for a loop this morning. It's nice to make your acquaintance as well, Mr. Connors. Or should I call you the Ghost?"

He laughed and clapped his hands. "Delightful. This is going to be even more fun than I had hoped."

Taking a seat at the table, Sydney made eye contact with Vaughn, who raised a questioning eyebrow. Without him saying a word, she understood his concerns: *What happened at the market? Are you all right?* She smiled reassuringly at him, letting him know that she was fine. His concern filled her with a warm, comforting feeling that wiped away the strangeness of the last few hours and brought her back down to earth. Sydney turned to Connors and smiled. "I'm sorry; I didn't mean to interrupt you. It sounded like you were in the middle of a story when I came in."

Connors seated himself next to Sydney and, somewhat disconcertingly, took her hand in his as he spoke. "I was just reminiscing with Arvin about a project that he and I were both peripherally involved in during the earliest days of his tenure in the intelligence field . . . although we never did have the pleasure of meeting face-to-face until today. You are familiar, of course, with the MK-ULTRA program?"

At the very mention of MK-ULTRA, Marshall let out a squeal of pleasure, then quickly clamped a hand over his own mouth.

Sydney, ignoring Marshall's outburst, nodded to Connors. "Of course. It was a series of CIA-backed mind-control experiments conducted in the fifties and sixties. Lots of LSD and assorted bad behavior. It tends to be very popular with conspiracy theorists."

Connors smiled and patted her hand. "Indeed it does. And Arvin spent a few months of his CIA infancy helping to administer some of those experiments. As you entered, I was just starting to explain my involvement in the project. When I joined MK-ULTRA, they were at the end of fifteen years of increasingly bizarre experimentation, and my role was strictly—how should I put it?—behind the scenes. You see, in the final months of the project, what we were *actually* studying was the effect of the experiments on the men *conducting* those experiments. What appeared to be a never-ending series of tests involving strange drugs and electronic brain implants was in reality an attempt to gauge and measure the human capacity to inflict pain on fellow men."

A look of surprise crossed Sloane's face. Apparently this hidden agenda was news to him. "I was a test subject?"

Connors nodded and continued with his reminiscence. "And, although he and I never met, I considered Arvin to be one of our star subjects."

A derisive laugh from Sydney, and a muttered "no doubt" from Dixon—neither of whom had any trouble believing that Arvin Sloane would be a star at inflicting pain on others—prompted Connors to protest. "You misunderstand. In spite of your own troubled histories with Arvin, most of which I am aware of, I always found him to be a remarkably pragmatic man who never inflicted pain or cruelty simply for the sake of inflicting pain or cruelty. This was a man who did what needed to be done in any given circumstance, always thinking several moves ahead. Unfortunately, some of his colleagues of less, shall we say, penetrating intelligence were not so restrained, and the entire project collapsed in a whirlwind of scandal and accusations. Most of the records were destroyed and a great deal of nastiness was swept under various rugs."

Sydney balked at the man's defense of Sloane and at the casual way he discussed a project that sounded like nothing more than torture. Sensing her disapproval, Connors attempted to turn the tide back in his favor.

"Of course, all of this was a long time ago . . . before I truly understood the amount of suffering caused by the actions of men like myself. Today, when I think of the things that I was a part of, the horrors that I witnessed and, to my eternal shame, facilitated . . . it makes me physically ill."

Connors's eyes filled with tears and Sydney felt herself warming to him. In spite of the mind games, the strange speech, and the rather exaggerated mode of dress, Connors did seem to be completely genuine.

She changed the subject, hoping to let him off the hook. "What did you do after the collapse of the MK project? I've heard so many rumors, so much speculation about you over the years. I'd be curious to hear your version."

Connors finally let go of Sydney's hand, pulled a handkerchief from a breast pocket, and dabbed at his eyes as he resumed speaking. "I remained in the employ of the CIA for several more years, conducting a series of experiments of my own devising. It was during this period, during just such an experiment, that I met your father. We did not know each other for long, but I count my days with Jack as some of the most valuable in my life."

Sydney hated to ask, but just couldn't resist. "What sort of experiment? Or would I be better off not knowing?"

Connors smiled and reached out for Sydney's hand again. "Perhaps you should hear about it from your father. I'm sure he could tell that story better than I could."

Unable to contain himself any longer, Marshall blurted out, "I don't think anyone could tell a story better than you, sir."

Connors smiled. "Some stories need to be told by a parent, Master Flinkman. Someday, you will tell young Mitchell the story of your adventures, and, believe you me, nothing will mean more to him than the fact that he is hearing the tale from his father's own lips."

Marshall was practically quivering with excitement. "You know my son's name?"

"I know a great deal about all of you," Connors replied, "and I look forward to learning even more. I must say that your work as a team has been exemplary. Really, quite spectacular."

"Well," Sloane interjected, "perhaps it's time that we heard just what it is that you have in mind for us. I must say, Langley was not very forthcoming when they alerted me to your visit."

A short, wheezing laugh broke from Connors's mouth. Quickly stifling it, he replied to Sloane. "I'm not surprised. I do my best to tell Langley as little as possible regarding my activities. Fortunately, my work has been successful enough to warrant me a great deal of autonomy."

"Not to mention your blackmail files. I'm sure those help with the auton—" Everyone turned their heads toward Marshall, who immediately blushed a deep crimson. "That is . . . I've heard . . . you know . . . that you . . . have . . ."

Taking pity on his number one fan, Connors smiled. "And what, pray tell, is it that you have heard, Marshall? That I have an entire warehouse of incriminating photos and recorded phone calls and smoking guns of every shape and size on every world leader and person of power that you can think of?"

Sheepishly, Marshall nodded his head. "Um, basically, yeah," he answered.

Another laugh, deeper this time, shook Connors's frame. "Sometimes it helps to allow such rumors to flourish. In fact, sometimes it helps to spread them yourself. I'm afraid there is no warehouse. And, if you think about it, there is no need for one. A warehouse is a large, expensive, and terribly vulnerable thing. One could accomplish as much with a few carefully chosen items, as long as those items pertained to the right four or five people. You could replace your warehouse with something no larger than an average briefcase." Connors accompanied this last bit with a slight wave of his hand toward his own briefcase.

Marshall's eyes nearly burst from their sockets. "Can I see them? Please. I won't tell anyone what they are."

Laying a friendly hand on Marshall's shoulder, Weiss spoke up. "Marshall, he's teasing you."

"He's . . . oh. Right." The look of disappointment on Marshall's face was enough to elicit a round of laughter from the others around the table. It was at that moment that Jack Bristow, coffee mug in hand, entered the briefing room.

"There you are, Jack," Sloane called out. "Come say hello to an old friend. I believe that you've met the Ghost."

Connors stood and held out his hand. "Hello, Jack."

The sound of Jack's coffee mug shattering as it hit the briefing room floor drew the attention of agents across the bull pen. Looking up from their computers and files, they were treated to the unprecedented sight of Jack Bristow, the man with ice water in his veins, turning pale with fear. In fact, more than one of the agents who witnessed the event later remarked that Mr. Bristow looked as if he'd actually seen a ghost.

CHAPTER 4

"Arvin, you have to trust me. That man is more dangerous than you can possibly imagine."

Sydney had never seen her father in this condition. It was a good five minutes since he had entered the briefing room and encountered Connors, but the color had not yet returned to Jack's face. He was speaking with an urgency and intensity that Sydney recognized as the tone of someone begging for their life. There was no denying it—Jack Bristow was terrified.

Immediately after dropping his coffee, Jack

had pulled Sydney and Sloane out of the briefing room and into Sloane's office. Sydney looked through the glass walls back toward the briefing room. Nadia had joined the group around the table and was currently occupying the seat of honor next to Connors. Sydney noted that their fickle visitor had a firm grasp on Nadia's hands now. She could see Mark Baker, a junior agent at APO, sweeping up the shards of Jack's broken mug while Marshall continued his questioning of Connors. She let her eyes drift to Vaughn, who was listening to Connors reply to one of Marshall's queries.

Suddenly, as if he could sense Sydney's gaze from across the building, Vaughn looked up and into her eyes. He smiled, and it struck her that she still hadn't had a chance to talk to him today. She returned his smile, and then reluctantly pulled her attention away from the man she loved and back to the conversation at hand.

"I've never seen you like this before, Jack. What brought this on?" Sloane seemed to be every bit as troubled by Jack's reaction as Sydney was. What on earth could possibly be so bad as to strike fear into the heart of Jack Bristow?

"Listen to me, Arvin. We need to lock him

down. Right now. We need to isolate him completely, and then we need to figure out a way to dispose of him. Permanently."

"Dad, you can't be serious," Sydney gasped.

Nothing about Jack's demeanor suggested that he was anything but serious. "Sydney, promise me you'll stay away from that man. I don't want you anywhere near him."

Before Sydney could protest, Jack turned his attention back to Sloane. "Arvin, I'm serious. We need to isolate him at once. And we need to lock down anyone who has been in contact with him. We need to make sure that no one eats or drinks anything that has been anywhere near that man. And we need to run complete bio-scans and toxin-screening protocols on everyone in this—"

"Jack," Sloane finally cut him off, "you need to calm down. We are under orders from Langley to cooperate with this man, and unless I hear something concrete from you, something other than ranting and raving, I am obligated to follow those orders."

It aggravated Sydney to hear Arvin Sloane—the personification of all that is criminal and evil—talking about his obligation to follow orders, but she had to agree with him in this case. Her father *did* need to calm down and tell them exactly what, or who, they were dealing with. If Connors was as dangerous as Jack said, then reacting emotionally and rashly was the worst thing they could do. Laying a comforting hand on Jack's arm, she said, "Dad, just tell us what we're up against here."

The sound of her voice seemed to get through to Jack. He took a few deep breaths and then, in a normal voice that both Sydney and Sloane were relieved to hear, he began to speak. "I was an unwilling participant in one of his experiments more than thirty years ago. It was . . . not an experience that I wish to repeat. And I would very much like to protect my daughter and everyone else in this facility from having a similar experience."

Sloane addressed Jack with genuine sympathy. "Jack, I'm sorry. When the orders came through from Director Chase, I had no idea that you had been through"—Sloane paused, not quite sure how to continue—"that you'd been through *whatever* it is that you've been through. I can ask her to task another division with the assignment, but she implied that the orders originated from higher up. I don't know how receptive they're going to be to our request. Connors seems to have a lot of clout."

"Dad," Sydney spoke up, "we don't even know what the assignment is yet. Shouldn't we at least hear what he wants before we rush to judgment?"

Jack gave a clipped, bitter laugh. "'Assignment'? Don't you see? *We* are the assignment. No matter what he says . . . no matter what *Langley* says . . . the truth will be something different. And the ultimate objective will be to get inside our heads and pull us apart, piece by piece, and see what makes us tick."

Noting the edge of hysteria that was creeping back into Jack's voice, Sloane attempted to defuse the situation. "Perhaps it's just my own situation that makes me say this, but don't you think that it's possible that he is a changed man? It has been thirty years, Jack. Please tell me that you don't discount the possibility of genuine change in a person, or the possibility of redemption."

It never failed to turn Sydney's stomach to hear Sloane go on about "change" or "redemption." *You're not fooling anyone, Sloane,* she wanted to scream, but she bit her tongue and didn't say a thing.

"I don't discount the possibility of change,"

Jack said. "And redemption is not the sort of thing that I deal with. But I do know what I saw in Nha Trang, and I know that any man capable of causing that . . . carnage . . . is not someone for whom 'redemption' is particularly an issue."

Sloane looked puzzled. "Nha Trang? Connors was in Nha Trang?"

"Connors? Who's Connors? If you mean that man in there, he was calling himself Peterson at the time. But yes, he was there. He was with me in the jungle."

Nha Trang? What was my father doing there? What happened? An entire list of questions ran through Sydney's mind, but clearly this was not the time to press Jack for answers.

"Interesting" was Sloane's only comment. "What do you want me to do, Jack? Shall I call Director Chase?"

There was a long moment while Jack considered his reply. When he finally spoke, something in his voice had changed. The fear had been replaced with a steely determination. "No. Let's hear what it is he wants us to do. But I warn you, Arvin. At the first sign that things are not on the level, I'm going to put him down—permanently."

Sloane simply nodded, and the three of them turned to leave the office and return to the briefing room. On the way out the door, Sloane put his hand on Jack's shoulder, holding him back for a second. With Sydney out of earshot, he addressed Jack quietly. "Jack, it has always been my understanding that you were the only survivor of Nha Trang."

Jack looked across the bull pen toward the briefing room, where he could see the man who was calling himself Connors still holding forth to his rapt audience. "Yes. And until ten minutes ago, that was my understanding as well."

CHAPTER 5

"What about the Mind Eraser? Is it true that you developed a pill that could completely strip a person's mind of any and all memories? I hear that it left heads of state rolling around on the floor like babies." Marshall had been taking advantage of Sydney, Sloane, and Jack's absence to bombard Connors with a nonstop series of questions. Each and every rumor, no matter how ridiculous or far-fetched, was dragged screaming into the light and then quickly dispatched by Connors. It was beginning to seem, to Marshall's chagrin, that the Ghost was a creature entirely composed of rumors.

"Once again, Master Flinkman, it pains me to admit that this is simply not true. Although, I will confess to starting that particular rumor myself. It very handily served to create quite a bit of chaos within the halls of a certain South American government that shall remain unnamed. You are, to my knowledge, the first person to connect me to that particular escapade. Kudos to you, sir."

This validation from the man he admired above all others was enough to have Marshall positively beaming. He immediately dove back into his seemingly endless supply of Ghost-related trivia. "I've also heard that you have changed your identity so many times that even you don't remember what your real name is. Is that true?"

"I'm deceptive, Marshall, not delusional." Connors laughed and winked at Nadia, who couldn't help but wonder if he had somehow overheard her remark to Sydney earlier. "Of course I know my own name. And, believe it or not, that name happens to be Connors. And this particular assignment will mark the first time that I have operated under that name in more than thirty years. That, no doubt, will take a bit of getting used to."

Junior Agent Baker, who had quietly remained in the room after cleaning up Jack's coffee mug, spoke up at this point. "Where did the nickname come from? The Ghost, I mean. I've heard that it comes from your penchant for faking your own death. Is that true?"

Everyone turned to look at Baker, whose presence had gone basically undetected up to that point. It was an unwritten rule at APO that junior agents were better seen than heard . . . and even better when they were neither. As the most senior agent present, Dixon took it upon himself to chastise the younger man. "Mr. Baker—"

"Ah . . . so you're Junior Agent Baker," Connors interrupted. "I've heard about you. Mark, isn't it? From California? Top of your class at Langley, I hear. One to keep an eye on, they say. A pleasure to make your acquaintance, Junior Agent Baker."

Baker, who suffered from the same affliction as Marshall—obsessive Ghost-itis, as it were—practically burst with excitement. He struggled to speak, only managing to croak out a hoarse "Thank you, sir."

Across the room, Marshall's eyes shot jealous daggers at this competitor for his hero's attention.

Fortunately for Baker, Connors began speaking again and Marshall forgot that there was anyone else in the room.

"The Ghost . . . ," Connors began with a tone of weary resignation. "To be completely honest, it's not a name that I have ever been comfortable with. If the truth be told, I was always hoping to be known as the Shadow—I freely confess to a love for old-time radio plays—but that name never took hold, and I gave up long ago on any attempt to rectify the situation. Also, I must admit, the Ghost conjures certain associations that have proven to be beneficial on more than one occasion. Never underestimate the power of fear, my young friends. But, to answer your question, Junior Agent Baker . . . this supposed penchant for faking my own death had nothing to do with the appellation. That moniker actually arose from my old partner's ability to infiltrate any facility, no matter how secure, and leave again, completely undetected. The man was truly ghostlike. I've never seen anything like it . . . before or since."

Quickly, before Baker could get a word in, Marshall spoke. "Partner? No one has ever mentioned that you—I mean—I've never seen any record of—" Marshall stopped and collected himself. "You had a partner?" he finished lamely.

Connors smiled, knowing the effect his words would have. "The lack of information about my comrade-in-arms is due to the fact that you are the first to hear about it. No one else in the world is aware of the fact that the Ghost was, for a good many years, more than one person."

The simultaneous gasps of excitement from Marshall and Baker caused the others in the room to laugh out loud. "Easy, fellas," Weiss snickered. "You sound like you're going to need a cold shower."

Ignoring Weiss, Marshall spoke in a hushed, reverential tone. "What happened to him? Your partner?"

The smile on Connors's face faded away, and he grew noticeably less animated. He looked off into the distance for a moment before speaking. "He passed away. Cancer. I couldn't believe it. To see a man like that . . ." His voice grew quiet. "That was one death we definitely couldn't fake."

For just a few moments, Connors looked like an old, feeble man. Then, shaking it off, he continued with his story. "After my friend passed, I continued on with the work that we had begun together. The name stuck, the legends grew, and"—here Connors indicated Marshall and Baker with a wave of his hand—"men like yourselves have helped to keep me from fading away into complete obscurity. And for that, I must thank you both."

The embarrassing spectacle of Marshall and Baker blushing and stammering about their unworthiness was cut mercifully short by the return of Sloane and the Bristows. All business now, the head of APO dismissed the junior agent with a curt "Mr. Baker" and then took his seat at the head of the briefing table. As Baker scurried from the room, Sydney moved around the table to take a seat next to Vaughn. Jack remained standing near the door with one hand inside his suspiciously bulky-looking jacket pocket.

"So, Mr. Connors," Sloane addressed their visitor. "Let's hear about this assignment."

CHAPTER 6

"Where do I begin? I suppose that a little background is in order . . . a little history lesson to help set the scene." Connors's tone was different now: The strange sentence structure remained, but the effect was less playful. Sydney wasn't sure if this was simply a desire to get down to business, or if it had more to do with her father, who was watching every move that Connors made with a look that would turn the average man to stone. Connors didn't *seem* unduly upset by Jack's scrutiny, but Sydney did note that he scrupulously avoided making eye contact with her father. The fact that Jack rather obviously had his hidden right hand on a gun did nothing to lighten the mood in the room.

"After my tenure with the Central Intelligence Agency came to a rather abrupt close—the result of a tragically failed experiment, I'm afraid—I regrouped and set up shop as an independent consultant, working wherever, and with whomever, I chose. I retained some ties with the CIA, as well as other agencies, but only on a case-by-case basis. This allowed me the freedom to turn down assignments that I found ethically, or politically, distasteful, while still availing myself of government funding. Eventually I opened a facility in Switzerland, the Devereaux Clinic, where I have been researching and developing, among other things, new methods of information extraction for the last ten years."

"Information extraction? Do you mean torture?" The tone of Vaughn's voice made it clear that he had no patience for semantics when it came to matters of life and death. Sydney made a mental note to add that to her ever-growing list of things to love about Michael Vaughn.

"Torture? Not at all, Agent Vaughn. It was and

is my express goal to make torture obsolete. I have always found it to be a crude and barbaric enterprise—not to mention inhuman *and* inefficient. No, what I have tried to develop is a safe, quick, and infallible method of retrieving information from a subject who may not want or may not be able to provide it. Think of it: an interrogation method that would do no lasting damage to the subject, but would provide one hundred percent accurate results one hundred percent of the time. Think of the lives that could be saved, the destruction that could be avoided, if we were assured that our intelligence was always correct. It would be the dawning of a new era in the shadowy world that we"—Connors made a flamboyant sweeping gesture with his hand, including them all in his utopian vision—"live and work in. And I firmly believe that I have succeeded in realizing this dream."

At this point Connors paused, clearly expecting some kind of positive response from the others in the room. The seen-it-all agents of APO hardly reacted. Vaughn turned to Sydney and rolled his eyes, expressing his disbelief. She smiled, but something inside her wasn't so eager to dismiss

Connors's story. She'd seen a lot in the last few years, and if it had taught her anything, it was that there was occasionally some merit in even the most outlandish claims. As Connors resumed his narrative, Sydney refocused her attention on him.

"The main component of this method is the strategic use of an exceptionally powerful hallucinogen of my own devising . . . an organically derived compound that I call January. This compound, when used under the supervision of trained personnel, has yielded the most spectacular results. Not just with information extraction, but, far more importantly, in the retrieval of traumatically repressed memories and the recovery of amnesiacs. I have even had a series of promising successes with restoring some degree of relief to poor souls suffering from advanced senile dementia. The possible applications of January are limitless."

"So where do we fit in?" asked Dixon.

"It appears, Agent Dixon, that I have been nursing a viper. One of my protégés, or perhaps more than one, has seen fit to abscond with the formula for January and offer it up for sale to the highest bidder. Obviously my research failed to take into account the apparently irresistible lust for wealth and power that seems to follow in the footsteps of true scientific innovation with terrifying inevitability."

"So why not go to the DEA and warn them that this new hallucinogen is coming on the market?" Sloane asked. "This hardly seems to be the sort of thing that would require the involvement of this department."

Connors shook his head. "You misunderstand. January is not entering the market as a recreational drug. It is far too dangerous, too volatile to ever have much use in that area. No, Arvin . . . January is being sold as a chemical weapon, which is something that I never even considered as a possibility. This was, quite obviously, a failure of imagination on my part."

"And how efficient do you think it would be as a weapon?"

Connors swiveled in his chair to face Vaughn. "It would be very efficient, Agent Vaughn. Terrifyingly efficient, in fact. The compound is easily concentrated, and the amounts needed to have an effect are fairly miniscule. It can be inhaled, injected, or absorbed through the skin. And the symptoms set in almost instantly. By the time you were aware that there was a threat, it would be too late. I imagine that it would be a fairly simple matter to aerosolize a quantity of January and, with the aid of a small crop-dusting aircraft, drive the entire population of a fair sized city into a psychotic episode of epic proportions."

"Lasting how long?" Vaughn asked.

"Lasting for days . . . perhaps even weeks. It would depend on the amounts and the concentration, but the effects of January have proven to be remarkably long lasting. Without a controlled environment and the guidance of someone like myself, the subjects would fall prey to violent hallucinations and an overwhelming sense of danger. Anyone and everyone they encountered would be perceived as a deadly threat and the subject would react with corresponding violence. When the dust finally settled and their minds finally calmed, I seriously doubt that there would be much of a city left. You must trust me on this, ladies and gentlemen. January is more dangerous than you can possibly imagine."

Sydney spoke up at this point. "Why do you call it January?"

Connors smiled as though this were the question he had been waiting all day to answer. "Thank you, Sydney. I was hoping to get to that." He expanded his focus to take in the whole room, with the exception of Jack, who stood behind him. "As you are all no doubt aware, the month of January is named for the Roman god Janus, the appointed guardian of doorways and portals, and the patron of endings and beginnings. And that is what I have been striving to perfect: a doorway into the mind, an end to darkness, and a new light for those who need it."

As he spoke, Sydney noticed that Connors was toying with a heavy silver ring on his left hand. She recognized the two-faced visage that adorned the ring from a comparative mythology class that she had taken at school during her SD-6 years. She had been working for Sloane's black ops division of the CIA only to find out that it was actually a front for a large-scale criminal organization. Once she turned this information over to the authorities, she found herself working as a double agent—reporting back to Michael Vaughn at the *real* CIA. Not surprisingly, the symbolism of Janus had affected her deeply at the time. She still thought about the dual visage of the Roman god every now and then—whenever she reflected on the infuriating fact that the government had pardoned Sloane for his crimes and put him in charge of the very division that Sydney had joined. *I have to hide the face that wants to tear the son of a bitch in half,* she thought.

"Isn't Janus also the two-faced god of deception?" she asked, earning a muffled snort from Jack. It was the closest thing to a laugh that many of those at the table had ever heard from him.

Connors was unfazed by her question. "Yes, Sydney, he is indeed two-faced. I see that you noticed my ring. I have always considered Janus to be a fitting patron for all of us in this business . . . on the metaphorical level, at least."

Looking around the room, at Sloane and her father and this strange little man, Sydney couldn't help but feel that he had a good point . . . on the metaphorical level.

Taking advantage of the lull, Nadia looked up from the notes that she had been taking. "How do you know that January is being sold as a weapon?"

"An excellent question, Ms. Santos. May I call you Nadia?" Nadia shrugged. "Nadia, I have, through the years, cultivated a rather extensive network of informants—men and women who have provided me with intelligence that has proven time and again to be reliable. One such source, a man in London by the name of Hopkins, recently alerted me to the impending sale of a chemical that he thought I might be interested in. Once I heard the description, it became quite obvious that this substance was, in fact, January."

"Do you know where the sale is taking place?" Nadia asked.

A Cheshire cat-worthy grin spread across Connors's face. "As a matter of fact, I do. The chemical will be up for sale in two days in Mexico City, at the Leuba Arms Market."

A ripple of excitement ran through the room. Even Jack betrayed a flicker of interest at the mention of the arms market. Weiss was the first to speak up. "You're kidding, right? You expect us to believe that the Leuba Market really exists, and that you know where it's being held?"

Before Connors could reply, Marshall raised his hand and said, "Um, excuse me." Realizing that he wasn't in school, and that no one was going to call on him, he put down his hand and asked, "What's the Leuba Market?"

Turning to the head of the table, Connors asked permission of Sloane to answer the question. A nod from Sloane later, Connors turned back to Marshall. "The Leuba Arms Market, Mr. Flinkman, is a legendary floating bazaar of the finest wares that the international weapons trade has to offer. It is held twice a year, never in the same place, and is so exclusive and well protected that it is often believed to be nothing more than a myth—a little like myself. I must admit, I'm a little surprised that you claim to have never heard of it, Marshall. It seems to be right up your alley. The CIA and a handful of other intelligence agencies scattered across the globe have attempted to infiltrate the Leuba for years. It is essentially a farmer's market for weapons of mass destruction, patronized by terrorists, corrupt regimes, and the highest echelon of drug lords looking to stock their arsenals."

As he said the words "farmer's market," Connors looked across the table at Sydney and winked. She smiled at him, but, remembering her father's warning, felt a little uneasy about the situation. Vaughn, always alert to her moods, reached under the table and laid a comforting hand on her thigh. Syd reached down and entwined her fingers with his.

"I suppose that you're going to tell us that you have a plan for infiltrating the Leuba Market and retrieving January." Dixon did not sound at all convinced by Connors's story.

"As a matter of fact, Agent Dixon, I do have a plan. A two-pronged assault that, if all goes well, will result in the dismantling of the Leuba, the recovery of January, and the unmasking of those responsible for its theft." Connors paused briefly for effect, then continued laying out his plan before Marshall could interrupt with a question. "The first part of the plan involves Agent Santos impersonating the daughter of a recently murdered Latin American drug lord in order to infiltrate the Leuba. I imagine that she will be supported in the field by you, Agent Dixon. Agents Vaughn and Weiss will also be on the scene, having taken the place of two members of a particularly violent and loathsome gang of white supremacists. My only regret is that I will not be able to be on hand to observe what promises to be a most entertaining operation."

Before she had even asked the question, Sydney

was already dreading the answer. "And the second part of your plan?"

Connors looked across the table at her and smiled. "Ah . . . that's where it gets interesting," he said. "Sydney and I will travel, in alias, to the clinic in Switzerland. . . ."

CHAPTER 7

"Sydney, I'm worried about your father. In all of the years that I've known him, this sort of behavior is . . . unprecedented." Sloane was obviously baffled by and genuinely concerned about Jack's recent actions.

It was thirty minutes since Connors had begun to outline the second half of his plan, but what a thirty minutes they had been.

As soon as the words "Sydney and I will travel, in alias, to the clinic in Switzerland" had left Connors's mouth, Jack had launched himself at the man. His outstretched hands wrapped around

Connors's throat, toppling his chair and propelling him backward to the floor. Keeping one hand on Connors's throat, crushing his windpipe and preventing him from crying out, Jack reached for the gun in his pocket. The other agents in the room had a moment of stunned inaction before snapping out of it and rushing to Connors's aid. It took the combined efforts of Vaughn, Dixon, and Weiss to subdue Jack and wrest the gun from his grip. During the struggle, Jack managed to fire a shot that narrowly missed Connors's ear and embedded itself in the briefing room floor.

The commotion drew the attention of agents all across the bull pen, including the armed guards who were stationed near the APO entrance tunnel. Two of the guards rushed into the room, weapons drawn, and were met by the strange sight of a furious Jack Bristow being held down by his fellow agents.

It had taken a while to sort everything out. Jack had refused to calm down—not even Sydney could get through to him—and had to be handcuffed. The guards led him to an interrogation cell, where he would be secured until further notice from Sloane. As he was led away, Jack had kept up a steady stream of shouted warnings to Sydney, mixed with obscenely colorful threats of what he was going to do to Connors if the man so much as looked at his daughter.

Connors appeared to be uninjured, save for a hoarse voice and a bit of bruising on the throat, but, just to be on the safe side, Marshall and Nadia accompanied him to the infirmary to get checked out. Sloane tasked Dixon, Vaughn, and Weiss to try to gather any intelligence that might corroborate Connors's assertion that the Leuba Market was to be held in Mexico City in a few days, and then asked Sydney to join him in his office.

A few minutes later, Sloane was expressing his concerns about Jack's "unprecedented" behavior. Every fiber of Sydney's being revolted at the thought of agreeing with Sloane on anything, but she found herself nodding her head.

"It's strange. I've never seen him react so emotionally to anything. Not even my mother's betrayal set him off like this." She hesitated a moment, then asked, "What was Nha Trang? That's a city in Vietnam, isn't it? I've never heard him mention it before."

Sloane nodded his head. "I'm not surprised. He and I have barely even spoken about it, until today. I will say this: Your father came back from that mission a changed man. Something had . . . hardened inside him."

"What do you know about it?"

"Nha Trang was a covert operation, late in the Vietnam War, led by your father. It was early in his intelligence career, the first mission under his command, and it was massively compromised. Everyone on the team, with the exception of Jack and apparently Mr. Connors, was killed. That's everything I know about it. I'm not even sure what their objective was. It remains the only significant failure in your father's career."

Sydney laughed, somewhat bitterly. "Unless you count getting conned into falling in love with and marrying a Russian double agent who proceeded to compromise your entire agency a failure."

"Your father's marriage to Irina resulted in you, Sydney," Sloane said quietly. "I don't think he would ever consider it a failure."

I really wish he wouldn't do that, Sydney thought. Shaking off the compliment, she tried to refocus on their current situation. "What do we do now? You said that Langley was pretty adamant that we work with Connors."

Holding his hands in front of his face, fingers steepled, Sloane thought for a moment. When he finally spoke, it was with great deliberation, and he chose his words very carefully. "Sydney, you know how highly I value Jack's opinion. There is no one I trust more in this world to make the sane, rational decision in any situation—no matter how difficult that decision may be. That being said, I don't think that we can rely on your father to make rational decisions in this instance. He is obviously traumatized by something, some event, to the point of being a liability to this team. Would you agree?"

"I'm incredibly conflicted here," Sydney said. "The one thing that I know for a fact about my father is that he would move heaven and earth to protect me." *Or put a bullet in the head of the woman he loved,* she thought. "But . . . as much as I hate to say it, I think that you're right. He's not thinking or acting rationally. And it's affecting him physically. Normally, if my father had wanted to kill Connors . . ."

Sloane finished her thought for her. "The man would have been dead before any of us could react. Yes, I thought of that as well. Let me ask you this: What do you think of Connors and his story?"

She took a moment before answering and couldn't help feeling a little disloyal to her father when she finally spoke. "I like him. He might be a little odd, but I think he's sincere and genuinely remorseful. And if this drug January is what he says it is, then we need to make sure that it's contained. I also think that the possibility of taking down the Leuba Market is far too attractive to pass up."

"Yes, it is attractive. I'm sure your father would say that its attractiveness is exactly why Connors offered it up—as bait for his trap. But I'm inclined to agree with you. I was concerned that my . . . personal situation . . . might make me overly sympathetic to someone claiming to be reformed and struggling for redemption. I'm reassured to hear that you felt the same."

Sydney briefly considered jumping across Sloane's desk and tearing his eyes out—at the very least she would get to spend some quality time with her father in the interrogation cell—but decided against it. *I promised Nadia that I would give Sloane a chance,* she thought, and brought her anger down to a simmer. "So, what's our next move?"

"Let's go talk to Connors—find out a little more about this Devereaux Clinic."

CHAPTER 8

SYDNEY'S HOUSE

"I bought a bunch of stuff at the farmer's market this morning. I was planning on cooking for you tonight." Sydney reached across the table and grabbed another dumpling with her chopsticks. "The best laid plans of mice and spies, huh?"

Vaughn smiled and shoveled some more fried rice onto his plate. "I can hardly blame you for not wanting to cook after a day like this. I keep thinking that it must be a full moon."

"Yeah, or Mercury's in retrograde or something like that."

It was late. Nadia and Weiss had gone out to a diner, but Syd and Vaughn had opted for take-out Chinese food and some time to themselves. Back at Sydney's place they had opened a bottle of wine and attacked the food, the first that either of them had eaten since that morning.

They ate in comfortable silence for a few minutes before engaging in a heated chopstick swordfight over the last dumpling. Vaughn let Sydney win.

After dinner they refilled their wine glasses and then curled up together on the sofa. They had a lot to discuss, but Sydney wasn't ready to spoil things just yet. A few minutes, a few kisses . . . surely APO could spare her that much time.

Eventually Vaughn raised his lips from hers and smiled. "I hate to be the one to break the mood, but . . . what the hell happened today?"

"Pretty strange, wasn't it?" Sydney sat up, already regretting that the kissing portion of the evening seemed to be over for the moment. "I can't believe that you had to help physically restrain my father. Dixon actually had him in a chokehold. That was so . . . weird."

"Yeah, and it's even weirder that we're still alive to talk about it. Did you get a chance to talk to him?"

She shook her head. "I tried to. He just told me to stay away from Connors and refused to say anything else. I have no idea what to make of any of this. Tomorrow I'm supposed to fly to Switzerland with a man who seems like a complete teddy bear, but is apparently the only person on earth that my father has ever been afraid of."

The plan to expose the thief, as outlined by Connors, involved Sydney and him traveling to his private clinic in Switzerland, disguised as a terminally ill father and his loving daughter. According to Connors, the clinic was a front for experiments that he ran from a remote location. None of the patients or staff had ever seen his face. He seemed convinced that the clinic's records, particularly the pharmacy logs, would give them the information that they needed.

Sydney snuggled underneath Vaughn's arm and rested her head against his chest, appreciating the fact that he at least seemed to be an island of normalcy in an otherwise completely bizarre world. "What's your take on Connors?" she asked, enjoying the rise and fall of Vaughn's chest as he breathed.

Vaughn stroked her hair while he answered.

"His information seems legit. A number of high profile targets, the kind of people that *would* be shopping at the Leuba, are either in Mexico City at the moment or have dropped out of sight and are presumed to be traveling. Plus . . . I don't know. I just kind of . . . *liked* him. He's fascinating."

"I know what you mean. I liked him too. I just feel weird about the whole thing. With my dad, I mean. Sloane thinks we need to keep him locked up until after the mission is over, for his own sake as much as Connors's."

"And what do you think?"

"I think that I like it when you play with my hair."

"I think that you're avoiding the question."

She sighed; it was not an easy question for her to answer. "I hate to say it, but I think Sloane's right. I think that unless he gives us something more substantial to go on, more than just this paranoid ranting and raving, then we have to assume that my father is a risk to himself and others. I think that we need to keep him locked up until I get back from Switzerland."

Vaughn laughed. "Jack Bristow and 'ranting and raving' in the same sentence. Not exactly 'milk and cookies,' you know what I mean?"

"How about ham and eggs?" she asked him with a kiss.

"Or maybe peanut butter and jelly," he countered, returning the favor.

Suddenly the kissing portion of the evening seemed to be back, full force. Sydney was just about to suggest moving the party to another room when, inevitably, the phone rang. At this hour, it could only be APO. She sat up, straightening her clothes. "How did that get unbuttoned? Very cheeky, Agent Vaughn." She picked up her cell and answered. "Hello?" She listened for a moment, hung up without signing off, then turned to Vaughn and broke the bad news. "I have to go. Apparently my father is ready to talk to me. Rain check?"

He sighed, knowing that nothing could convince Sydney to stay. "Okay, I'll take the rain check, but don't try to get out of it. I know where you live."

CHAPTER 9

APO HEADQUARTERS

"Thank you for coming. After what happened earlier . . . I wasn't entirely sure that you would."

Sydney sat across from her father in the cold, sterile cell. A cot had been brought in and there was a small table with two chairs, but other than that, the room was empty. The walls were completely white, with the exception of a two-way mirror. Sloane had cleared the observation room and promised Sydney that her conversation with Jack would not be recorded. She believed him. Jack's handcuffs had been removed, but there were armed guards posted outside the door.

"Of course I came. I'm worried about you."

"I can see why you might be. I'm sorry about that. I got quite a shock this afternoon, seeing that man. But I can assure you, I'm fine."

She was relieved to hear him speak; he sounded like himself. That afternoon's wild-eyed prophet of doom seemed to have vanished. "I'm glad to hear it," she said. "Do you want to tell me what all that was about?"

He shifted nervously in his chair and Sydney realized that things weren't exactly back to normal. Jack Bristow *never* shifted nervously in his chair. When he spoke, she could hear the panic in his voice, lurking just beneath the surface. "There is not much in this world that frightens me." He paused, and Sydney could tell that he was struggling to stay calm. "Basically, only two things frighten me—two things that I'm aware of. One is the idea that some harm will come to you. It is a fear that I have to deal with, every minute of every day. But I do deal with it. The work that we do demands it." He stopped, unsure of how to continue.

"And the second thing?" Sydney gently prompted him.

"The second thing . . . the second thing is not being in control of my own actions. The very thought of surrendering to my baser instincts, of making decisions based solely on my emotions . . ." He didn't finish the sentence. "Fortunately this has rarely been a problem."

"You didn't seem to be in control this afternoon."

"No. I wasn't. And the last time that I was so thoroughly out of control was the last time I saw that man."

"Was that the Nha Trang mission?" she asked quietly. He nodded, but didn't say anything. "Do you want to tell me about it?"

After a long pause, Jack finally answered. "I don't. I'm sorry, but I don't think I can talk about it."

Sydney was trying to be sympathetic to her father's feelings, but she was hurt that he thought there was something, anything, that he couldn't talk to her about after all they had been through in the past few years. She stood up to leave. "I should go. I have to pack."

He reached across the table and took her hand, holding it gently. Sydney felt his pulse racing, and his hand trembled slightly. She was a little taken aback. Her father was not normally a hand holder. When he spoke, he looked her directly in the eye. "Sydney, please, don't go on this mission. I don't know what he's up to, but I promise you, it isn't what it seems. He is using you and Sloane and this entire team for some other purpose. Some *experiment.*" Jack practically spat out the last word. "And it will not end well. Please." His shoulders slumped and he dropped her hand. He had given it his best shot.

Sydney sat back down, knowing that he would answer her now. "Dad, do you want to tell me about Nha Trang?"

When he finally began to speak, he kept his eyes on the floor, as if he were too ashamed to look at her. "It was 1971 . . . ," he began.

VIETNAM, 1971

Five men dressed in green camo that matched the lush vegetation of southern Vietnam's central highlands made their way slowly, single file, up the rocky side of a steep mountain in the minutes just before sunset. It had been raining nonstop for four days—not at all uncommon for mid-August—and they were all soaked to the skin. Water poured off their rain ponchos in rivulets, and all but one of the men carried a heavy pack on his back.

The large man at the back of the line, a battle-scarred mercenary by the name of Hutchins, shielded his eyes from the water and looked back across the densely forested valley that they had spent the day crossing. It was starting to get dark, but along the western horizon the clouds were breaking up a bit and the rays of the setting sun cut across the valley.

They had made good time over the past few days, considering that they'd stayed off of trails and had to cut their way through the jungle every step of the way. Hutchins reckoned that they were now a good ninety kilometers inland from their starting point, the coastal city of Nha Trang. That meant that they would most likely camp somewhere near the target's compound tonight—hopefully not *too* close—and strike sometime around dawn. Any luck at all and they'd be calling the choppers for extraction by lunchtime tomorrow . . . provided the man in charge didn't do something stupid and get them all killed. *Man? Hell,* boy *is more like it. Twenty-one years old and they have him leading a mission into the jungle to take out a guy like Nguyen Quang? Goddamn pencil pushers. What the hell are they thinking?* Knowing that there was nothing to be gained by that train of thought, Hutchins shrugged his pack up higher onto his shoulders and concentrated on working his way around a moss-slicked outcropping of stone.

Ahead of Hutchins in line were Martin and Lewis, army-trained snipers on their first mission for Intelligence. Best friends since second grade, they had managed to stick together through basic training and their first few months in-country. People tended to laugh at the boys when they first met them, and not just because their names were—really—Martin and Lewis; they were ridiculously gung-ho, and more than a little naive—they had actually fallen for the old "the word *gullible* is not in the dictionary" gag—but the laughter stopped as soon as the boys picked up their weapons. Martin and Lewis were amazing marksmen, and spookily efficient to boot. When faced with multiple targets, the boys would dispatch them in record time, without wasting a bullet or exchanging a word. The constant rain had dampened everything but their spirits, and they remained excited and flattered to have been chosen for the mission.

In front of Martin and Lewis was the wild card: a strange little man, the only one of the party not struggling beneath the weight of a heavy pack, named Peterson. None of the other team members had met Peterson before their rendezvous in Nha Trang four days earlier. Hutchins, who was very insistent on knowing the men he was working with, had done some digging and come up almost completely empty handed. He managed to learn that Peterson was thirty-five years old but seemed much older, and that he had an annoying way of speaking. Other than that, Peterson was a complete mystery. Hutchins had tried talking to him on their first night in camp, only to realize later that he had learned exactly nothing about Peterson and had revealed the entirety of his own life story. After that, Hutchins left the little guy alone. *Spooky bastard. Something ain't right about that guy.*

As they crested the mountain, the man at the front of the line held his hand up for the team to stop. He took advantage of the last few minutes of daylight to survey the box canyon that stretched out below them. This was the purported stronghold of their target, a local warlord by the name of Nguyen Quang. Quang was a common thief who'd had no political leanings until the North Vietnamese Army had brought him into the fold with the winning combination of guns and money. Since then, he had been carrying out a campaign of terror against U.S. and South Vietnamese interests, helping to pave the way for the North. It was the team's objective to locate and neutralize Quang—and anyone with him.

The man at the front of the group could just make out the smoke of two small fires at the far end of the canyon, most likely sentry posts, but no sign of Quang's compound itself. Aerial reconnaissance photos of the area had been completely useless—the jungle in this region was just too thick. He would have to trust that their intel was correct and that the target was holed up somewhere in the jungle below them with a dozen or so followers. The plan was to make their way down the mountain and camp for a few hours on the jungle floor in preparation for a predawn raid on the compound. After a quick look to confirm that all five of their party had made it to the top, Jack Bristow shouldered his pack and waved for the others to follow him down the slope.

* * *

It took the better part of two hours to make their way down to the jungle floor, by which time the rain had begun to let up. The clouds started to break up a bit and the full moon helped to illuminate the team's way. The timing was fortuitous: They were too close to their target to light a fire tonight, but at least they weren't completely in the dark.

A short way into the jungle, no more than a few hundred yards, Jack held up his hand to halt the team. This was far enough. The vegetation wasn't quite as thick here—they were on the edge of a small clearing—and enough moonlight filtered through the branches for them to see what they were doing. Without a word, they shrugged off their packs and dropped to the ground, happy to be off their feet for the first time since morning.

The relief was short lived. Jack only gave the team five minutes to rest, during which time he scouted out the driest spot he could find and then waved for them to join him. They assembled at the base of the large tree where Jack had dropped his pack and waited for his orders.

"Martin, you're on perimeter," Jack spoke quietly. "I want a full three-sixty sweep. Make sure we aren't moving into the wrong neighborhood here."

The young man nodded, and then asked, "Can I take Lewis with me?"

"Go ahead. Take five to eat something, and then I want you both out there."

Both men nodded this time, in comically precise unison, and then moved off to where their packs were waiting. They weren't exactly looking forward to the meal of dried meat and fruit, but Peterson had slipped them a bar of good old American milk chocolate to split for desert. Martin and Lewis definitely thought that Peterson was a weird old bird, but he was okay in their book.

Hutchins laughed softly as the young soldiers moved away. "If only the real Dean and Jerry had got along as well as those two, eh, Bristow?"

Jack's face betrayed no sign of amusement. "I'm sorry, Mr. Hutchins. . . . Who are Dean and Jerry?"

"Oh, come on, Bristow. Martin and Lewis? Dean and Jerry? Why do you think people laugh at those yokels?" He might as well have been talking to a wall. "Are you kidding me? You don't know who Dean and Jerry are? Where do you come from?" Hutchins looked to Peterson for support but was met with nothing more than a shrug and an enigmatic smile . . . not that Hutchins knew the meaning of the word *enigmatic.* "Incredible—the both of you," he muttered.

"While I'm sure that Dean and Jerry, whoever they might be, are completely fascinating," Jack said, "right now I suggest that you forget about them, check your weapons, and try to get some sleep. You're on second watch."

Hutchins bummed one of Peterson's little cigars and then moved off, more than happy to get away from the pair of freaks. *Who the hell doesn't know who Dean and Jerry are?* he thought. Hutchins flopped down near his pack, a good twenty feet from Bristow and Peterson—not far enough, if you asked him—and set about field stripping and cleaning his CAR-15 assault rifle.

As Hutchins walked away, Jack allowed himself a slight smile. The humorless, granite-faced front that he projected had served Jack well. He was moving up the ladder quickly, being given assignments, like the present operation that probably should have gone to older, more experienced operatives. He recognized that there was a social toll to pay—not a lot of nights out with the boys—but he was more than willing to make the sacrifice.

Especially when "the boys" were shifty, gun-for-hire types like Hutchins. Earlier in the week, Jack had been forced to physically restrain the mercenary from beating a Vietnamese prostitute over a disagreement related to the price of her services.

"You know damn well who Dean and Jerry are." Peterson was smiling as he spoke, keeping his voice low enough that Hutchins wouldn't be able to hear.

"Maybe. But I would gladly pretend not to know who Richard Nixon was if it would keep me out of a conversation with Hutchins," Jack admitted. "Besides, I'm more of a Laurel and Hardy man, myself."

"It was always the Marx Brothers for me. You and I are not completely in step with the times, I'm afraid," Peterson replied. "Still, I can't say that I blame you for not wanting to chew the fat with Hutchins. Our mercenary friend has not exactly endeared himself to me, though I will confess to a certain fondness and admiration for the other two. Loyalty like that is a rare and precious commodity in this world."

Jack agreed wholeheartedly with Peterson's assessment of Martin and Lewis and told him so. He was glad to have Peterson along on the mission . . . though he hadn't felt that way at first. When originally given command of the operation, it had been made clear to Jack that he was *not* going to be allowed to choose his own team—definitely not the ideal situation. He had no problem with Martin and Lewis, but Hutchins was grade-A scum—an animal without conscience or remorse that killed strictly for money and had been known to switch sides at the slightest hint of a fatter pay-check. Jack could only assume that there was a serious shortage of special-ops troops available at this point in the war.

Peterson's presence on the team was a bit of a puzzle. In fact, *Peterson* was a bit of a puzzle. As far as Jack could tell, the man was unarmed. He only carried a small pack—really it was more of a knapsack—that couldn't have held much more than four or five days' rations . . . although he seemed to have a never-ending supply of thin cigars that smelled vaguely of cinnamon when smoked. He barely slept at all, and then only sitting up . . . his back propped against a tree, wrapped in a water-proof tarp that Jack had loaned him after the first night. It was obvious that he wasn't a military man, and Jack had never heard mention of him in the intelligence community. In the days before the mission, Jack had contacted Arvin Sloane, one of the few men in this world that Jack trusted completely, and had him try to dig up something on Peterson. It was to no avail. All that Jack knew was that the powers that be wanted Peterson on the mission, and they had specifically charged Jack with making sure that no harm came to the man.

Jack had been prepared for Peterson to be a burden, fully expecting that the strange little man would be unable to keep up and would slow them down. If he were a betting man, Jack would have wagered that Peterson wouldn't even last through the first day. But Peterson proved to be remarkably resilient. He kept pace and never once complained. Good thing, too. Hutchins did enough complaining for all five of them put together. But Jack's opinion of Peterson was cemented in camp the first night when the man had walked over, sat down next to him, and suggested a game of chess.

Now, just a few short hours before they would reach Quang's compound, Jack suggested, "A quick game? I believe that you're first up."

It had become their nightly ritual: a feat of

mental prowess that would have taxed the brains of most men to their breaking points, but left these two feeling relaxed. Martin and Lewis had been completely mystified, and Hutchins, being the kind of man that he was, had assumed that Bristow and Peterson were "blowing smoke." He could not have been more wrong.

"King's pawn to E-four," Peterson opened.

Jack countered, "Pawn to E-five," and the game was on.

The play was astonishingly rapid, considering that the board existed solely in their minds. The two men were almost perfectly matched, although Jack had a tendency toward aggression that sometimes tripped him up. He leaned back against the trunk of the tree, closed his eyes, and stripped and cleaned his rifle while hammering away at Peterson's defenses. For his part, Peterson smoked a cigar and toyed with the bulky ring, which featured a strange engraving of a head with two faces, on his left hand. When Martin checked in with an "all clear" twenty minutes later, they had played three games in quick succession and Jack was up two to one.

Eventually they grew tired and settled down to

get some sleep. Jack carried a vibrating, windup alarm that he set as a precaution, but he knew from experience that he would wake ten minutes before it went off. He happily split a bar of Belgian dark chocolate with Peterson—*Where does he keep it all?* he had wondered—and then drifted off to sleep, enjoying the smell of his friend's cigar.

A terrifying shriek rang out through the jungle and Jack Bristow was instantly awake, rifle in hand. A quick glance at the luminous dial of his watch told him it was just after midnight—he had been asleep for less than two hours. The moonlight was not as strong as it had been earlier, but there was still enough to see by.

A branch snapped to Jack's left. He spun toward the sound, ready to fire, but recognized Peterson. He nodded to his chess partner, relieved to note that the other man held a Walther PPK in his right hand. *Not unarmed after all,* Jack thought. *Good man.*

Jack cocked his head toward where Martin and Lewis had been sleeping. Peterson nodded and followed after Jack, both of them straining to see into the darkness. The moonlight gave a strange, silvery hue to the jungle, and every shadow was filled with menace.

Martin was in a slight dip in between two exposed tree roots and Jack didn't see him until he almost tripped over the younger man's boot. For a moment, it was too dark to tell if Martin was dead or sleeping, but then a cloud passed from in front of the moon and the night grew a little brighter.

Peterson immediately staggered backward, then turned his head and vomited. Jack clenched his teeth and fought down the wave of nausea that threatened to overwhelm him. Gaining control over his stomach, he knelt down to get a better look at the body.

The moon was reflected in pools of blood and viscera, and there was steam rising from the cavity that had once held Martin's stomach and intestines. His throat was sliced, down to the bone, and his eyes and tongue had been cut out.

Jack rose and crossed to Peterson. "Are you all right?" he asked.

Peterson wiped his mouth with the back of his hand and shook his head. "No, but I will be. What do we do?"

Jack took stock of their situation. "Hutchins

and Lewis are missing. We haven't heard any gunfire. And . . . that"—he gestured toward the body—"looks more like the work of a psychopath than a soldier."

"How could someone have butchered that boy without us hearing a sound? It doesn't make any sense." Peterson was shaking his head, and over the next few seconds kept muttering "it doesn't make any sense" over and over. He seemed to be in shock.

"Keep it together, Peterson. We need to find the others and regroup. Can I count on you?"

Peterson looked at Jack, seeming to draw strength from the younger man's resolve. "Yes. We need to find the others. Quickly. Which way do you think we should look?"

Before Jack could answer, a single gunshot, followed by an agonized scream, rang out from deeper in the jungle. "That was Lewis screaming," Jack said. He was already running toward the noise as he called back over his shoulder. "Follow me. Keep your gun ready." All thought of remaining quiet had vanished, replaced by an urgent desire to save their comrade.

They ran through the jungle as fast as the

moonlight would allow. Jack was surefooted and quick, and Peterson did his best to keep up. Another scream pierced the darkness, this time louder and more drawn out. Jack veered left, following the sound. "This way," he shouted.

They ran in silence for a few minutes and Peterson was beginning to wonder if they hadn't gone the wrong way. Suddenly Jack came to a dead stop. Peterson skidded to a halt, almost crashing into Jack's back. They were on the edge of a large clearing. In the moonlight, Peterson could just make out a hulking stone structure in front of them. He recognized the architecture by its shape—the distinctive towers and pillars of a Hindu temple. It was a remnant of the kingdom of Champa that had ruled Central Vietnam until the sixteenth century. The decaying edifice was completely overgrown with vines and seemed like it might crumble at any moment. Peterson could make out several large shapes, silhouetted against the moon, moving across the temple facade. He raised his pistol, but Jack laid a comforting hand on his arm. "Monkeys," he whispered.

Jack slung his rifle over his shoulder and unholstered his .45 automatic. He motioned for

Peterson to follow. They stepped out of the trees and into the clearing just as another scream split the night—much closer this time. Hundreds of birds lifted off from the underbrush and tree branches, and a deafening cry went up from the monkeys that made their home in the ruined temple. After a few seconds, the noise subsided and an eerie quiet returned to the jungle.

Jack and Peterson circled the ruins slowly, constantly turning, ready for an ambush. They had just worked their way around to the back of the temple when a gap in the clouds opened up, allowing them a better view of their surroundings. Peterson gasped, drawing Jack's attention, and pointed to something sprawled on top of a pile of rubble about ten feet in front of them.

It was Lewis. His arms and legs were twisted into impossible positions and the hilt of a large hunting knife was protruding from his chest. His eyes were wide open and his face was frozen in an expression of complete terror.

Jack couldn't tear his eyes away from the sight of Lewis's body. Something was wrong . . . something that he couldn't put his finger on. An incessant buzzing in his ears drew Jack's attention.

How long has that been going on? he wondered, swatting at the air around his head. "Damn mosquitoes."

"Jack," Peterson hissed, eyeing Jack warily. "We have to find Hutchins. He's gone completely mad."

Ignoring Peterson, Jack pulled his rifle from his shoulder and set it on the ground. He bent down to get a closer look at the body. "Look," Jack said, pointing at Lewis. "Look at his arms."

The dead man's arms were coated in blood and gore up to the elbows. His left fist was clutching a grisly trophy: a human tongue. Peterson glanced at the body but didn't seem at all surprised by what he saw. When he spoke, his voice was very calm. "I know," he said. "Lewis killed Martin. Come with me, Jack. It's very important that we find Hutchins immediately."

"I feel . . . strange," Jack murmured, clutching at the rubble for support as a wave of dizziness swept over him.

"I know you do, Jack. I can help you through this. You just need to listen to me and try to stay calm."

Jack turned to face Peterson. Something about

the man's voice had changed. Even his face, only half visible in the moonlight, looked different . . . sinister somehow. Everything about this situation was wrong: the way that Peterson was speaking, the buzzing sound, and now the searing pain behind Jack's eyes. He tried to raise his pistol and point it at Peterson, convinced that the other man was somehow behind what was happening, but he was struck by a blinding bolt of pain. Jack clutched his head and reeled backward. "Peterson, what's happening to—"

He didn't get a chance to finish the question. With a terrifying roar, Hutchins burst out of the jungle a few yards away and rushed at Jack, his outstretched hands bloodied and curled into claws.

Hutchins hit Jack at full speed, driving him to the ground. Jack's instincts kicked in, overriding the pain in his head, and he twisted as he fell, using Hutchins's momentum against him. They rolled as they hit the ground and Jack pushed Hutchins away, losing his grip on his pistol in the process. Both men scrambled to their feet and immediately rushed at each other again. They slammed together and Hutchins, being the larger of the two, drove Jack backward while clawing at his face. Jack caught Hutchins's wrists and fought to keep the other man from tearing out his eyes. As he was propelled backward, the heel of Jack's boot caught on a crack between two slabs of stone and he fell with Hutchins right on top of him. Jack's head smashed into a flat slab of stone with a sickening thud and he fought to retain consciousness.

The pain infuriated Jack and gave him an incredible burst of energy. Roaring like an animal, Jack wrapped his leg around Hutchins's for leverage and rolled over, getting the other man beneath him. Jack could feel blood gushing from a wound on his scalp, and from somewhere, it sounded very far away, he could hear Peterson yelling at him to move out of the way. But there was no stopping him. He used the weight of his entire upper body to bear down on Hutchins's left wrist until he felt it snap beneath him. Jack let go of his enemy's now-useless hand and reached for the blade he kept strapped to his ankle. As he pulled the knife from its sheath, Jack had a split-second of clarity: *This is not right. I am not in control here.*

Hutchins, sensing an opening, raised his head and sunk his teeth into Jack's wrist. With a roar, Jack brought the knife up and plunged it into

Hutchins's chest. He immediately pulled it out and brought it down again . . . and again.

When he was finally finished with Hutchins, Jack stood up, bloody knife in hand. He turned to face Peterson, who stood a few yards away with his gun pointed right at Jack.

"Jack, you have to listen to me," Peterson said, and Jack noted that his voice was no longer calm. Peterson was terrified. "I know what's happening. I can help you."

Jack just smiled and raised the knife. "Come here, Peterson," he said.

Sydney could see how hard it was for her father to talk about this. His words came slowly, as if he had to force every last one of them to leave his lips. His eyes never left the floor and his hands were still slightly trembling. Sydney had never seen him so vulnerable.

"Peterson tried to calm me down, but it was no use." Jack's voice was just barely above a whisper now. "I killed him. In cold blood, while he begged for his life. I stabbed him in the heart . . . twice."

Sydney was confused. *How could my father have killed Peterson, if Peterson is Connors?* But she didn't want to interrupt.

"Eventually, I'm not really sure how, I made it back to our camp," Jack continued. "I retrieved my pack and started hiking north, determined to complete the mission. Obviously I wasn't thinking straight. I came across Quang's old compound sometime around noon. It was quite evident that it had been abandoned for months."

"The mission was completely bogus?" Sydney asked.

Jack nodded. "I spent months, years actually, trying to find out what we were really doing out there, but I never got very far. I did manage to learn that we had been part of a larger psy-ops experiment testing the use of hallucinogens in high-stress environments—an experiment initiated by someone called the Ghost—but that was it. I was never completely sure of what had actually happened out there and what I had hallucinated. It never occurred to me that Peterson had actually been the one responsible . . . that he was the Ghost."

"Until this afternoon," Sydney said.

"Until this afternoon," Jack agreed, "when everything fell into place." He looked up at her now, his face clearly displaying the guilt he felt. "I have lived with this for all these years, and it never gets any easier."

"But Dad, you didn't kill him. Obviously it was just part of the hallucination."

Jack's reply was immediate and forceful. "Him? I wish I *had* killed him. I could have stopped him from turning people into guinea pigs, from running these ridiculous, inhuman experiments. I don't think that man deserves to live." Jack's eyes welled up as he admitted the true source of his guilt. "No . . . it was the others. Those boys, Martin and Lewis, were under my command. Their lives were my responsibility, and they died horribly, without reason."

"Dad, maybe you should talk to Connors—"

Jack held up his hand, cutting her off. "It's not necessary," he said. "I know that I reacted . . . improperly . . . today. I can't explain it. It was as if I were back in that jungle, back at that temple. And I know that you are going to go on this mission, in spite of anything I might say." Knowing he was right, Sydney looked away, unable to meet his eyes.

Jack reached across the table and once again took her hands in his. "Sydney, I know that you want to believe that people are capable of change, of redeeming themselves. That belief is part of what makes you who you are, and I wouldn't change that for the world. But you and I both know that there are people in this world who will exploit those characteristics and turn them against you. Please. Be careful. I'm begging you."

Sydney's eyes filled with tears as she nodded her head. They both stood up, and Sydney hugged her father and kissed him on the cheek before turning to leave. She called for the guard to open the door as Jack sat back down at the table.

As she left, he called her name. She turned back to him, and he smiled sadly. "Don't forget," he said. "No matter how much you believe that you are in control of what's happening . . . you are mistaken."

CHAPTER 10

MEXICO CITY, 12 HOURS LATER

The torero waved his purple and yellow cape with a dramatic flourish and the half-ton bull snorted and charged. The crowd, a mere twenty thousand strong in an arena that could hold upward of sixty thousand, roared with excitement. The bull, the second of three that would face the matadors that day, was fast and agile. This promised to be a good fight.

"See how this guy just stays out of the way, doesn't do anything fancy?" Weiss asked. "That's because he's a . . ." Weiss set aside the bottle of water that he was drinking from and consulted his pocket guide to the bullfights. "He's a torero. That's like an assistant matador. He's not allowed to show off or anything. He's just there to display the bull so that the real matador can see what he's up against."

"I can relate," Vaughn said, keeping his eyes trained on the two men that he and Weiss were tailing.

The APO agents were dressed like American college students in Bermuda shorts and T-shirts and were seated in a section of the arena warmed by the afternoon sun. They had a perfect vantage point from which to enjoy the spectacle and pageantry of the bullfight—and the spectacle and pageantry of the Jerk Brothers.

Their targets were seated five rows below Vaughn and Weiss, and didn't seem to be enjoying the spectacle and pageantry at all. They were both clad in classic biker chic: leather, denim, boots, and chains. Their names were Crawford and Burnett, more commonly known to their friends as Diesel and Snake. But they had lately been rechristened Big Jerk and Little Jerk by Agent Weiss.

They were members of the Brotherhood of the

Shining Night, a particularly virulent and loathsome gang of "racial purists" that had recently sprung up in the Pacific Northwest. Vaughn had been suspicious of their presence at the market—they seemed a little too small-time to wrangle an invitation to the Leuba—but Connors had assured them that the Shining Night had big money behind them and that they were definitely an emerging threat.

The group hadn't made much of a splash yet—they were much better at getting drunk and fighting with one another than they were at planning and executing large-scale acts of terror—but their two highest ranking members being in Mexico City for the Leuba Arms Market seemed to indicate bigger plans for the future.

The APO team had tailed the men from their hotel on Paseo de la Reforma, near the entrance to Chapultepec Park, to the legendary Monumental Plaza Mexico, which was purported to be the largest bullfighting ring in the world. They had watched in disgust as Big Jerk and Little Jerk loudly insulted or argued with nearly everyone they encountered, starting with the doorman at the hotel, and then proceeding to the cab driver, the ticket takers at the bullring, and the old men selling beer to the crowd. Now they watched as the pair removed their T-shirts and sprawled across two sets of bleachers, catcalling to the matadors and generally behaving as obnoxiously as possible.

Weiss had always wanted to see a bullfight and was taking full advantage of the situation. He studied the guide that he had purchased from a vendor in the plaza in front of the bullring and kept up a running narration of the afternoon's program to Vaughn, who *had* seen a bullfight before, and was anything but a fan.

"You have to look at it from a cultural perspective," Weiss insisted. "This is seen as a display of bravery and machismo on the part of the matadors. It's steeped in tradition," he concluded, quoting more or less directly from the guide.

Vaughn gave a noncommittal grunt and kept his attention on their quarry.

A trumpet blast announced the next stage of the bullfight and two men on horseback, the picadors, entered the ring carrying colorfully decorated sticks with sharp, metal tips. When the first one pierced the neck of the bull and stuck, an enormous cry of approval went up from the crowd.

"Sounds like it's getting exciting in there," Nadia's voice sounded in Weiss and Vaughn's ears. "How are our racist friends enjoying the afternoon?"

Weiss watched one of the men, Big Jerk, spit out a wad of tobacco juice that splashed the shoes of a well-dressed woman several feet away. As she moved away in disgust, Weiss answered Nadia. "Oh, they're having a great old time. Definitely the ugliest of ugly Americans."

"Sorry I'm missing it. Tell me again why Outrigger and I are stuck out here in the van while you two are getting suntans and drinking beer?"

Weiss laughed and took a drink from the bottle of water, gulping loudly for Nadia's benefit. "We're out here and you're in there because you guys lost the coin toss. And just for the record . . . the beers are merely a prop to help us blend in." He winked at Vaughn. "I'm not enjoying them at all."

"You see, that's the problem with you American guys," Nadia said in a teasing voice. "You like to decide things with a coin toss. In Argentina, we would have decided things much more professionally."

"Oh, really? And how would you have decided things in Argentina?"

"Rock, paper, scissors, of course. It's really the only civilized choice."

Vaughn spoke up. "Evergreen, you can take my place. I've had enough bullfighting to last a lifetime. What's your twenty? I'll come meet you."

At that moment, deciding that they too had seen enough bullfighting to last a lifetime, Big and Little Jerk stood up and started making their way to the exit located at the bottom of the bleachers. Vaughn saw them first and gave Weiss, who was engrossed in the bullfight, a nudge.

"Change of plans, Evergreen. Targets are on the move," Vaughn said quietly into his comm.

"Could be they're just headed to *los baños*," said Weiss, mangling the pronunciation.

"I don't know," Vaughn replied. "They don't really look like the type of guys who make trips to the bathroom together. We should be ready for them to exit the stadium."

"But there's still another fight left," Weiss protested.

"Tell that to the Brotherhood." Vaughn stood up as the men reached the bottom of the bleachers and entered the tunnel that would take them beneath the seats and out to the main concourse. "Come on," he called to Weiss, and hurried down the stairs.

In the van, Dixon turned the ignition key and started the engine. "We're good to go, Shotgun. I'm parked on the boulevard, right across from the main entrance plaza."

Vaughn and Weiss rushed through the tunnel and reached the concourse—just in time to see their targets walking past the line for the bathrooms and making a beeline for the main gates. "Copy that, Outrigger. They're definitely headed for the exit. I'm guessing they'll grab a cab. Be ready to follow."

They trailed the men as they exited through the red iron gates, underneath a large arch topped by a magnificent sculpture of charging bulls, and pushed their way rudely through a crowd of vendors that waited outside the Plaza. "Here we go, Outrigger. Targets approaching the street."

Dixon looked through his windshield, then checked his mirrors and grimaced. "I hope they pick a slower cab than the one they came here in. This traffic is ridiculous."

Big and Little Jerk approached the main street leading away from the bullring, but instead of flagging down a cab, turned left and began walking down the sidewalk.

"Outrigger, they're on foot. Headed west, away from you."

Dixon looked at his passenger-side mirror. "I have a visual, Shotgun. They're probably headed for the San Antonio subway station. I'll try to swing this thing around and get ahead of them. You should stick with them on foot."

Vaughn and Weiss fell into step behind the men, keeping a good half block back. "Copy that, Outrigger."

They were walking down a wide avenue with traffic running in both directions. The street was filled bumper-to-bumper with cars, more than half of which seemed to be Volkswagen Beetles, many of them painted the distinctive green and white of a Mexico City taxi. There were a good number of pedestrians on the sidewalk, but not so many that Vaughn and Weiss felt comfortable with getting closer to their targets.

The Jerks approached a pedestrian overpass and started up the concrete stairs. Vaughn immediately alerted Dixon. "They're crossing over to the other side, Outrigger. Have you managed to get turned around?" At that moment, a chorus of angry car horns sounded from behind Vaughn and Weiss. Noting that they could hear the horns through their comms as well, they both laughed.

"We'll assume that means no," snickered Weiss.

Dixon was too busy cranking the wheel of the large black van and hopping the center median to reply. Nadia, hanging on for dear life, managed to get out a terse "We're working on it."

Weiss and Vaughn were climbing the stairs of the overpass, keeping an eye on the two men who were already halfway across. Big Jerk paused for a moment to spit tobacco juice on the cars passing below and then scurried to catch up with his friend.

Dixon, ignoring another volley of horns, finally got the van turned around and heading in the right direction. "We're turned around, Shotgun—although I think about half of the drivers in Mexico City want to kill me."

"Copy that." Vaughn held up his hand for Weiss to stop for a second. They were at the halfway point and the Jerks were just starting down the stairs on the other side. Vaughn was looking at the street ahead of them, a plan forming in his head. "Outrigger, the next two blocks are pretty open. See if you can get ahead of the Jerk Brothers and pull over somewhere. Maybe we can take them now, save ourselves a few hours of following these idiots around."

"Copy that, Shotgun. I'll see what I can do."

Vaughn and Weiss picked up the pace a little. The two men they were following had reached the opposite sidewalk now and were continuing toward the subway station.

As the agents walked, trying to close the gap between themselves and the men ahead, Weiss asked Vaughn a question that had been on his mind all afternoon. "Do you think that the lightning bolt is striking the book, or is the book shooting out a lightning bolt?"

Vaughn pondered the logo of the Brotherhood of the Shining Night that was stitched in golden thread on the back of both the Jerks' jackets. "I'm not really sure," he replied. "I'd be surprised if Tweedle-dumb and Tweedle-dumber even knew what a book *was*."

In the van, Dixon spied a space along the curb large enough for the van but not very far in front of the Jerks. "Shotgun, I've got an opening just ahead . . . right past that bread truck. Can we move that quickly?"

Vaughn watched as Little Jerk snatched a bag of peanuts from a stooped old woman pushing a vending cart and threw them into the street, much to the amusement of Big Jerk. "Yeah," answered Vaughn. "We can do it. Let's get these monkeys off the street."

Vaughn and Weiss moved quickly, closing the distance between themselves and the Jerks in less than half a block. Just as the Jerks were drawing alongside the waiting van, Weiss piped up, addressing Big Jerk. "Hey man, is this the way to the subway?"

Big Jerk turned and sized up Weiss before answering. *Looks like a couple of goddamn college students, but hell . . . at least they're white,* he thought. "Yeah, it's right up there. Just be ready to be stuffed into a train with a buncha these greasers."

"Why don't you take a cab then?" Vaughn asked. "There seems to be plenty of them around."

Little Jerk laughed and spit on the ground. "The

cabs are even worse. Any white face is an invitation to robbery down here."

Weiss gritted his teeth. This was going to be a pleasure. "I'd like to thank you guys," he said.

"What for?" asked Big Jerk.

"For making this next part easy," Weiss said as he drove his fist into the big man's chin. He followed the uppercut with a surprisingly fast and graceful spin, driving his elbow into the side of Big Jerk's head. The big guy dropped to the ground, out like a light.

Little Jerk, reactions slowed by an afternoon of nonstop beer drinking, was just reaching for the knife he had strapped to his hip when Vaughn grabbed his wrist and spun him around, twisting his arm violently up between his shoulder blades. Behind Vaughn, the old peanut vendor laughed and clapped her hands in approval.

The side door of the black van slid open and suddenly Little Jerk was face-to-face with his worst nightmare: a black man and a Hispanic woman pointing automatic weapons at him.

"Nice spin you had there," Vaughn commented as Weiss pulled a groggy Big Jerk to his feet.

"Thanks. I've been practicing," Weiss replied as they propelled their captives toward the curb.

Dixon smiled and stepped aside as Vaughn and Weiss roughly bundled the two men into the van. *"Bienvenidos a México, amigos,"* he said.

CHAPTER 11

SWITZERLAND, 11 P.M.

Sydney knew that the train from Zurich was traveling through some of the most beautiful country she had ever seen: rolling green hills dotted with picturesque villages against breathtaking mountain vistas in the distance. The only trouble was that it was pitch black outside, and all she could see was her own face reflected in the window pane. She had been to Switzerland before, several times, and each time she was amazed at what a lovely place it was. As she stared at her reflection, she reminded herself that she needed to visit some of these places when she wasn't working . . . preferably with Vaughn along for company.

The thought of Vaughn made her smile. She pulled her sweater tighter around her shoulders and closed her eyes, imagining a time when she and Vaughn could actually take a trip together. Her reverie was interrupted by Connors returning to their compartment with two bottles of water and a bar of dark chocolate.

"I thought that a little of the local specialty was in order. Will you join me?" Connors, resplendent as always in seersucker accessorized with a white rose, removed his jacket and settled in for the journey.

She smiled and accepted the water and half the chocolate bar. "Thank you," she said, before remembering her father's words of warning. A shadow of doubt crossed her face, and she set the water and chocolate on the seat beside her. "I'll save mine for later," she said.

If Connors was offended, he gave no sign of it. "Fine," he said. "I suppose we should take this time to fill in the blanks a little. We haven't had much chance to talk."

It was true. There hadn't been much prep time

in Los Angeles, so they had worked straight through the night, arranging transportation, manufacturing documentation that matched their aliases, and gathering the equipment that they would need. They had slept through most of the flight to Switzerland and then rushed straight to the train station. Now they were rumbling through the darkened countryside, expecting to arrive in the village of Taviston sometime in the late morning. From there, it was a thirty-minute cab ride to the clinic, which was perched on a wooded hill overlooking Lake Lucerne.

The compartment that they occupied was big enough for six people, with two benches facing each other and luggage racks above, but so far they had it to themselves. Connors sat across from Sydney, prepared to answer her questions.

She already knew the basics: They were traveling as a Mr. Reginald Connors and his daughter Sydney. He had laughed at her gentle suggestion that an alias was intended to mask one's true identity . . . and that perhaps using their real names was not the best way to go about that. "My dear Sydney," he had replied. "It has been years since I was in the field. Undoubtedly I would get things mixed up and call you by your true name anyway. This way, we avoid any mistakes."

Their cover story was simple. Mr. Connors had supposedly been diagnosed with lung cancer and subsequently refused to accept any treatment. His loving daughter was escorting him to the clinic, where he would spend his few remaining months living a life of luxury in a physically beautiful setting. So far, so good, but Sydney wanted a few more details.

"Tell me more about the Devereaux. What can we expect when we get there?"

Connors nibbled at the chocolate bar as he spoke, stopping every now and then to take a drink of water. "I founded the clinic almost ten years ago, but it has been quite some time since I actually set foot on the grounds—more than five years, I believe. It will be interesting to see the old place. It was quite beautiful, as I remember."

"And the staff?" Sydney asked. "Could any of them recognize you?"

"Not a one," Connors replied. "Over the years, I have managed to swap out the old guard completely. We will have complete anonymity."

"What about the patients? Are they mostly

terminal, like my poor, dear father?" she asked playfully.

"There are two levels to what goes on at the Devereaux. The day-to-day operation of the clinic is completely legitimate, and amazingly lucrative. Extremely wealthy families from all over the world send us their castoffs. Any family member who has become a liability or an embarrassment is shipped off to Switzerland, where, for an exorbitant amount of money, we provide them with as much comfort as is humanly possible."

"What sort of liability are you talking about?" Sydney asked.

"Terminal illness, Alzheimer's, dementia, physical deformities, you name it. We house patients displaying physical and mental disorders of every stripe. The families that I speak of—and believe me, you would recognize their names—would do anything to keep their more unfortunate relations out of the public eye. I truly believe that they look on the natural process of aging as a sign of weakness, and if plastic surgery can't cover it up, then it must be concealed in some other fashion." Connors's voice had taken on an angry, bitter tone that Sydney hadn't heard in it before. "It amazes me that people are so afraid of this aspect of life—so afraid that they would hide it away somewhere rather than look it in the eye and try to understand it. Death and decay are a part of life, and no amount of running from that is going to change things."

Sydney could see that something very personal was fueling Connors's anger, but decided against questioning him about it. "You said that there were two levels to the clinic's operation?" she prompted him.

The inquiry seemed to bring Connors back from the dark side. "I'm sorry," he said. "I tend to get a little worked up about certain topics. Forgive me." Sydney nodded, and he continued filling in the missing pieces of the situation at the clinic. "Yes, as I said, there is a second level to the Devereaux, a set of patients who have come to the facility through the auspices of my work with the international intelligence communities. These patients tend to be a deeply wounded lot: amnesiacs, shell-shocked combatants, agents whose minds have snapped due to torture. They are men and women who have been traumatized and brutalized in the service of one country or another and then discarded by those same countries. Ten years ago, I let it be known to my circle of contacts that the Devereaux would welcome these poor souls, free of financial and political considerations, and that we would try to comfort them the best we can. No names, no records. The outrageous sums that we charge the 'legitimate' patients also pay for these others . . . the shadow patients, as I have come to call them."

"That sounds very noble," Sydney said, "but I suppose that these shadow patients also make excellent subjects for your experiments."

He smiled, but Sydney could see that her skepticism hurt him. He looked her in the eyes and spoke quietly, with great feeling. "I can appreciate why you would think that, Sydney. But I assure you, it has been many, many years since I conducted my experimentation in anything but the safest and most controlled of environments. And I have not caused any harm to come to a single one of my subjects, either knowingly or accidentally, in all that time. Believe me, if I thought that there was the slightest risk of harm coming to these people, I would cease and desist at once. I will never again be responsible for . . . that kind of thing."

"I'm sorry, I didn't mean to offend you," she assured him, then attempted to steer the conversation in a different direction. "You said before that these experiments are all run by you, but without any direct contact. How does that work?"

"It's quite simple, really. I have a home in Italy, in a beautiful little village called Cifani, and my office there is networked to the clinic's computers. I have a high-speed video connection and all of the experimental sessions are broadcast directly to me. I make all decisions regarding treatment, dosages, and experimental settings. My voice is piped directly into the treatment rooms so that I can 'guide' the patients through their sessions." He smiled and laughed. "Pay no attention to the man behind the curtain, I believe the saying goes."

"It sounds like it would be a lot simpler just to conduct the experiments yourself."

"It would be, very much so . . . but past experiences have left me terribly gun-shy when it comes to this work. I firmly believe in the value of what I'm doing, but I find that I can only remain objective and efficient if I approach it with some degree of separation. It adds an extra layer of difficulty, but the separation is a safety blanket that I am not prepared to give up."

She nodded, but found herself having a hard time imagining this gregarious man isolating himself from anybody. And she couldn't help wondering if the "past experiences" he mentioned included the Nha Trang mission . . . and if he'd be willing to talk about that at some point.

"Sydney, there is something that I'd like you to understand." His eyes never wavered, and he spoke with complete conviction. "It is only by aiding these unfortunates that I can begin to make up for the terrible things that I have done in this life. I hope, if nothing else comes of this operation, that you will walk away knowing that I am completely sincere in my belief that helping these people is my salvation—my redemption."

Sydney held Connors's gaze and, despite the warning voice of her father echoing in her ears, found herself believing every word that he said.

CHAPTER 12

MEXICO CITY

"Don't you think that if you were making a major illegal arms buy at six in the morning you'd want to turn in? Maybe get a good night's sleep so you'd be fresh for all the haggling over the price of grenades and what not?" Weiss had to speak loudly to be heard over the din of the nonstop club hits that were being pumped through the massive speakers that ringed the room. When he didn't get a response from his fellow agents, Weiss's shoulders slumped and he resigned himself to the fact that there wasn't going to be a lot of sleeping tonight.

The APO team was seated at a table in a smoky, dimly lit Mexico City nightclub, keeping an eye on the beautiful Marta Mendoza as she danced and drank the night away. It was well after midnight and Ms. Mendoza showed no sign of slowing down. The team had tracked her and her bodyguard from their hotel, a far more luxurious one than that occupied by Big and Little Jerk, to Club Perilous more than three hours earlier. Since that time, they had been discreetly observing as she downed one margarita after another.

"How does she do it? I'd have been to the restroom five times by now," observed Vaughn, who was seated next to Dixon. Weiss and Nadia sat together on the other side of their table. The plan was to wait until Marta went to the ladies' room, where Nadia would secure her while the guys took care of the bodyguard. It was a risky move in a crowded nightclub, but they hadn't had time to prepare anything more elaborate.

"The only thing she goes through faster than tequila is dance partners," remarked Nadia as Marta snagged a passing gentleman and dragged him—with very little resistance—to the center of the dance floor.

There was certainly no shortage of men for Marta to dance with. She was a gorgeous girl with straight black hair that hung all the way down her back, beautiful dark eyes, and a lush, full mouth. She was dressed in a tight, low-cut black dress and was wearing impossibly high-heeled boots. She danced seductively with all of her partners, but never kept one around for a second song.

"I think I must be getting old," Dixon said. "I look at that girl, and all I can think is, what if that was *my* daughter?"

"If that was your daughter, you'd be one of the biggest cocaine traffickers in the world," Weiss said. "And you'd be dead."

Ms. Mendoza was the daughter of the late Bartolomeo—popularly known as "Lucky"—Mendoza. Lucky, who was never called that to his face, had run a massively successful drug smuggling operation. He had acquired the nickname by managing to avoid arrest, as well as multiple assassination attempts, for more than twenty years. His luck had finally run out two months earlier, when a rival cartel contrived to gun him down as he was leaving his favorite restaurant.

Mendoza's daughter, not being particularly

business-minded, had turned over the operation of her father's empire to her uncle Ricardo and devoted herself to the glamorous life . . . and avenging her father's murder. According to the latest intelligence, she had already identified the guilty parties and was now busily seeking a suitably colorful method with which to dispatch them. She had made the trip to the Leuba Market—an event that her late father had attended religiously—in the hopes that she would find something to inspire her.

"What's our good friend Günther up to?" Nadia inquired.

Over Nadia's shoulder, Vaughn could see the improbably named Günther Hathaway, Marta's personal bodyguard, glowering as his charge began grinding against the latest in her never-ending string of admirers.

"Just keeping an eye on things," answered Vaughn. "He looks like a fun guy, doesn't he?"

"You see? He and I *do* have a lot in common," laughed Dixon.

The plan for tomorrow morning's operation at the Leuba Arms Market called for Nadia and Dixon to pose as Marta Mendoza and her bodyguard, while Vaughn and Weiss took the place of what

Weiss now referred to as the Brotherhood of Ignorant Jerks. It was a good plan, the sort of thing that they did all the time, but there was a hitch: If anyone at the market had a description of Günther, they were sunk.

Connors's intelligence had indicated that Marta Mendoza always traveled with a bodyguard named David Fox, a six-foot Londoner of Nigerian extraction. The plan had been set in motion based on the idea that Dixon would impersonate Fox. Unfortunately, as they learned during a phone call from Marshall after they'd landed in Mexico City, Fox had broken his leg playing soccer two days earlier. Marta had been forced to bring her late father's head of security, Günther Hathaway.

Günther was not a tall man, barely over five feet with his stack heel shoes, and he was of mixed German, Irish, and Scottish heritage. His awareness of fashion trends had apparently ceased sometime in 1977, and he accessorized his white polyester suit with an impressive array of gold chains and a near-lethal dose of cheap cologne. He was built like a bulldog and had a face and personality to match. Dixon was an incredible mimic, but he was nowhere *near* good enough to pull this off.

"Maybe I should go to the market alone. Why risk blowing the whole operation?" asked Nadia.

Dixon gave it some thought before answering. "I think that's even riskier. No one shows up at that place alone. Plus they know that the Mendoza family has two daggers."

The daggers were the keys to entering the Leuba market. They were small, about four inches long, and elaborately jeweled. Each of the daggers was unique, and the gatekeepers at the Leuba were trained to recognize them on sight. According to Connors, all they would have to do to enter the market was flash the dagger and identify themselves with the appropriate names. They had already relieved the Brotherhood of Ignorant Jerks—presently cooling their heels in a holding cell at the U.S. embassy—of their daggers; tonight's objective was to secure Marta and Günther and acquire theirs. They were just going to have to gamble that no one knew what Günther was supposed to look like.

"Heads up," said Vaughn. "Our girl is headed this way."

"It's about time," said Nadia. "I was starting to think that she wasn't human."

As Marta walked by their table on the way to the ladies lounge, she stared at Vaughn with undisguised interest. Her eyes traveled over every visible inch of his body, and it was quite clear that she liked what she saw. Her tongue snaked out and ran across her bottom lip as she passed. Günther, following a few feet behind Marta, also looked at Vaughn . . . but not quite in the same way.

"Did Günther actually just growl at me?" Vaughn asked when the bodyguard had passed.

"I'd say it was more of a snarl than a growl," Weiss replied. "But did you see how *she* looked at you? That was . . . amazing."

"Change of plans," said Nadia, sensing an opportunity. "You need to ask her to dance. See if you can't get her out of here, back to the hotel."

The suggestion seemed to make Vaughn instantly uncomfortable. "No way. You've seen how she works: one dance and you're done. We're just wasting time. We should take them now."

"Nadia's right," said Dixon. "Maybe we can get them away from here. It would be a lot safer than risking a takedown in this place."

"What makes you people think that I'm going to have any more luck than the last twenty guys?"

Dixon laughed. "She's just been checking out the menu up until now. We all saw the way she looked at you. I'd say she's definitely ready to order."

"You guys, please don't make me do this," Vaughn begged.

"Don't make you do this?" said an incredulous Weiss. "What is wrong with you? That girl is volcanically hot."

Nadia raised an eyebrow. "Oh," she said teasingly, "is she your type?"

"Volcanically hot South American girls are *exactly* my type," Weiss replied, putting his arm around a laughing Nadia.

"Come on, Michael," Nadia said, enjoying Vaughn's discomfort immensely. "Sydney and I are constantly having to parade around in tiny little outfits, using our feminine wiles to get to the bad guys. Let's see some masculine wiles for a change."

"I'm pretty sure I don't have any masculine wiles. Particularly not any that would interest this girl . . . unless she's really into hockey."

Marta walked by their table, eyes locked on Vaughn the entire time. As she passed, she trailed her finger along Vaughn's arm. The invitation was unmistakable. Günther followed in her wake, looking as though he'd like to tear Vaughn's arm off and beat him to death with it.

"You need to be careful," Weiss laughed. "I think that the growler is a wee bit jealous of you."

"Great," Vaughn sighed. "Do I really have to do this?"

"Oh yeah," said Dixon. "It's time to get your groove on."

"I'm glad that you guys find this so amusing," Vaughn said as he reached into his jacket pocket and removed his communications earpiece. "Just don't blame me when it all goes terribly wrong," he warned as he slotted the tiny device into his ear. The others followed suit and discreetly donned their comms.

"Go get her, tiger," Nadia said with an enormous smile.

Vaughn stood up and crossed the room, headed for Marta's table, like a man walking to his own execution.

"There he goes," Weiss said, for the benefit of the table as well as Vaughn, who could hear him via comms, "Agent Double-Oh-Smooth."

"You aren't helping," hissed Vaughn through clenched teeth.

When she saw Vaughn approaching, Marta's eyes lit up and her lips spread into a wicked, triumphant grin. Weiss kept up his running commentary. "Why, Agent Shotgun, is that a pistol in your pocket or are you just happy to—"

"Eric, stop it," Nadia interrupted, although she seemed to be amused. "Let the man work his magic."

Vaughn wasn't exactly sure which magic it was that Nadia was referring to. He had reached Marta's table and still hadn't decided on an opening move. He stood in front of her for a few seconds, not saying anything, while she stared at him expectantly. She seemed amused by his silence.

Finally, without saying a word, Vaughn held out his hand to her. Her smile grew even wider and she placed her hand in his. He turned around and led her out to the dance floor, where he spun her around and then quickly drew her in close to his body and began to dance with her. He barely moved at all, just gently swaying back and forth, but he looked deeply into her eyes and allowed her to press against him.

"Okay," said Dixon, impressed. "*That* was smooth."

Back at Marta's table, Günther's eyes shot flaming rays of death in Vaughn's general direction. "Looks like Günther's not too pleased with your dirty dance moves, Swayze," Weiss commented.

Nadia laughed. "Let's not get too carried away here, Shotgun. You know I promised my sister a full report when we get back."

Suddenly a familiar voice chimed in through their earpieces. "Hey, guys," Marshall said. "What is the girl wearing? Is she as hot as she looked in the surveillance photos?"

Before he could stop himself, Vaughn rolled his eyes in exasperation.

"Is something wrong?" Marta asked in Spanish.

Quickly recovering, Vaughn smiled and shook his head. He recalled from Marta's dossier that she had attended school in Massachusetts, and he replied in English. "I was just thinking, now that we both have what we came here for, we should move the party to my hotel—unless you think that your boyfriend will object."

She didn't even hesitate before replying in lightly accented English. "Boyfriend? Hardly. He's no problem. Günther does what he's told. But we better make it *my* hotel. I have an early appointment tomorrow and there are some things I'm going to need."

"That's got to be the daggers, Shotgun," Dixon interjected. "We'll track you and wait for you to call in the strike before we move."

Vaughn smiled and answered Marta and Dixon simultaneously. "Perfect," he said.

In Vaughn's estimation, the cab ride back to Marta's hotel set a new record for awkward and uncomfortable situations. Günther sat up front with the driver, barking out directions to the hotel and constantly throwing angry looks at Vaughn over his shoulder. Marta kept running her hand up Vaughn's thigh, and Weiss and Marshall kept up a stream of inappropriate comments in his ear. It was the longest fifteen blocks of his life.

Finally, exasperated with his fellow agents and tired of wrestling with his amorous seatmate, Vaughn grabbed her wrist a little bit roughly and threatened her—and them—with bodily harm. "If you don't stop it, I'm going to have to give you a spanking." The prospect of a spanking from

Vaughn did nothing to cool Marta down—quite the opposite, in fact—but, strangely enough, brought complete silence from Weiss and Marshall.

They reached the hotel at last, a sleek modern tower in the heart of the Zona Rosa, and used a swipe card to access a private elevator from the lobby. Marta and Günther were staying in the penthouse suite, which occupied the entire top floor of the building.

The elevator ride was almost as uncomfortable as the cab, due to a bout of frenzied ear licking that could have turned disastrous had Marta targeted the ear with Vaughn's comm receiver. "Baby needs a spanking," she whispered in Vaughn's ear, and he couldn't help but worry that she had said it loud enough for his comrades to hear. He was relieved when his earpiece remained silent; there was no way that Weiss would have passed up an opportunity to comment on *that*.

The suite was beautiful. The large center room had glass walls on two sides, with spacious balconies that provided unparalleled views of the city. There were two bedrooms, a freestanding fireplace, a bar, a hot tub, and an enormous flat-screen television. The only thing that seemed to be missing, Vaughn was relieved to note, was any additional security personnel. "Just the three of us?" he said, for the benefit of the team on comms. "Cozy."

"Why don't you pour us a drink and then meet me in the bedroom? I'm going to change into something special for you." Marta didn't wait for Vaughn to reply. She turned and walked out of the room, slipping her dress from her shoulders as she went.

Vaughn walked to the bar, aware of the bodyguard's scrutiny every step of the way. He grabbed a couple of shot glasses and a bottle of tequila . . . and seriously considered downing one before making the move into the bedroom. He smiled at Günther and raised one of the shot glasses in salute. "Günther, isn't it? Do you want one of these before I get out of your hair?"

"Piss off," Günther growled, perhaps angered by the fact that he was completely bald and had no hair to get out of.

"No? Your loss, buddy." Vaughn laughed and crossed to the bedroom. As he was shutting the door, he addressed one last remark to the human bulldog. "You know, Günther, you remind me of my uncle Pete. He was a real charmer too."

In the hotel lobby, Dixon reacted to the word "uncle"—the signal to move in—and immediately responded to Vaughn on comms. "We're on our way, Shotgun . . . ETA five minutes."

The bedroom was completely dark, save for a sliver of light that crept in through the ajar bathroom door and sliced across the king-size canopy bed. "Where are you?" Vaughn called in a singsong voice, hoping that Dixon would recognize that the question was actually directed at him.

"We're taking the public elevators to the twenty-fourth floor and then using the emergency stairwell from there. Hang in there," Dixon answered just as the bathroom door was flung wide open and light spilled into the room.

"Here I am," Marta said, dramatically backlit as she posed in the doorway. "Do you like?"

Apparently her idea of "something special" to change into was . . . nothing. Vaughn gulped and tried to come up with a suitable reply. "I like," he said, not sounding particularly sincere, and held up the tequila and glasses. "Do *you* like?"

"I like very much," she purred, and crossed from the doorway to the foot of the bed, leaving the door open and the bathroom lights on. As she crawled catlike onto the enormous four-poster, Vaughn struggled to find a place to direct his gaze and finally settled on the floor. "Why don't you pour me one and bring it over here?" she asked.

Vaughn turned around and set the glasses on top of a dresser and opened the bottle, doing his best to ignore the voice of Marshall in his ear, who was wondering out loud if he could equip field agents with some kind of high-resolution video camera in the future.

Vaughn was thankful for the opportunity to turn away from Marta's undeniably spectacular nakedness for a moment, but he still had no idea how to play these next few minutes. He didn't want to knock the girl out—that hardly seemed appropriate. But he was afraid that if he just identified himself and told her that she was under arrest, she would call for Günther. Vaughn was unarmed and didn't fancy his chances against the bodyguard on his own. The only option that made sense was to play along with her until Dixon and the others took down the bulldog.

There had been times in his career (quite a few, actually) when Vaughn had to feign interest in one woman or another in order to complete a mission. It was never a part of the job that he particularly relished—much to Weiss's amazement and disbelief—but he never hesitated to do it. But lately, especially in the last few months, he had found it an almost impossible task to even look at a woman besides Sydney with anything but mild disinterest. She consumed his thoughts and passions to the exclusion of all others . . . even others who were naked, curled seductively on a nearby bed, and calling thirstily for tequila. *Hurry it up, Dixon,* he thought.

Steeling himself, Vaughn poured a shot for the girl and walked over to the side of the bed. He handed her the glass and watched her knock it back in one gulp, then toss the glass on the floor. As she reached for Vaughn, attempting to pull him down onto the bed with her, inspiration struck him. He pulled back, just out of her reach, and smiled. "Turn over and put your hands behind your back," he said as he pulled off his tie.

"Ooh, I like this game," she murmured as she rolled over and placed her hands on the small of her back, right above an ornate tattoo of a scorpion.

Vaughn knelt on the bed beside her and proceeded to bind her hands together using his tie, noting to himself ruefully that it had been a gift from Sydney. Marta purred gently, but didn't protest a bit. As far as she was concerned, things were moving along just fine. Just as Vaughn finished tying her hands and was starting to wonder what to do next—*Maybe I really should spank her*—he was saved by the bell. Or, more precisely, he was saved by a loud crash and an angry roar from Günther.

"What was that?" Marta squawked, attempting to sit up.

"My knights in shining armor," Vaughn answered while pressing her back down onto the bed with the flat of his hand. He grabbed one of her ankles and spun her around so that she was lying crossways across the bed, and then rolled her up into the heavy bedspread. As the sounds of a fight in the next room escalated, he unplugged a nearby floor lamp and then pulled the cord from the base. He quickly tied it around the squirming, screeching bundle on the bed—it wasn't much, but it would hold her for a few minutes—and ran to the bedroom door.

In the main room, Vaughn was greeted by the sight of Günther, Dixon, and Weiss rolling on the floor, surrounded by broken wood and glass. The short but powerful bodyguard had Weiss in a headlock with one arm while his other hand gripped Dixon's throat. Vaughn's fellow agents were not making much progress in their struggle with the human bulldog, who was even stronger than he looked. Nadia was standing nearby, silenced pistol drawn, but couldn't get a shot off for fear of hitting one of her thrashing and kicking friends.

Vaughn, who was thoroughly fed up with the way the evening had progressed, crossed to the bar and grabbed a half-empty bottle of scotch. He walked over to the scrapping trio and brought the bottle down as hard as he could across the top of Günther's skull. The bottle shattered, dousing Weiss and Dixon in liquor, but the impact was enough to knock the bulldog out.

It took the team almost an hour to clothe and secure their prisoners, locate the two daggers, and tend to their own cuts and bruises. By the time that they had finished, the sun was about to come up over the eastern horizon. They had less than an hour before they were due at the Leuba Arms Market. Vaughn and Weiss needed to get back to the Brotherhood's hotel to change clothes and wait for their ride.

On their way out, Vaughn sighed as he surveyed

the beautiful hotel room that had been reduced to a disaster area by the fight with Günther. "What happened in here?" he asked Weiss. "I thought you had been practicing your moves."

"You're right," Weiss said, looking properly contrite for just a second before replacing the look with an evil grin. "I've been a bad boy," Weiss said, and Vaughn's shoulders slumped—he knew what was coming. "Baby needs a spanking," Weiss finished, to a chorus of laughter from Dixon and Nadia.

CHAPTER 13

SWITZERLAND

It was still pitch black outside the train window. Sydney knew that she should try to nap, even though she had slept on the flight over from America, but her mind was racing a thousand miles a minute. There was so much that she wanted to ask Connors, particularly in regards to the Nha Trang mission, but she had no idea how to broach the subject. She had long since set aside her fear and opened the chocolate that he had brought her. Now she unwrapped the last piece and popped it into her mouth. It was delicious.

Connors was engrossed in the latest issue of a European psychiatric journal, but, perhaps sensing that she wished to talk, looked up from the magazine and smiled warmly at Sydney. "Are you comfortable?" he asked. "Would you like a blanket?"

"I'm fine," she replied. She hesitated a moment, then decided to dive in. "I wanted to ask you . . . what was it exactly that made you decide to run your experiments remotely?" She stopped short of asking him about Nha Trang directly.

"You want to know if my decision had anything to do with what happened in Vietnam, with your father. Is that it?"

Sydney looked away, embarrassed, and Connors spoke up immediately. "Please, don't be embarrassed. I assumed that your father would tell you what happened. I'd be very curious to know what he said. I've never been sure what it was, exactly, that he believes took place out there."

She wasn't quite sure how to answer at first. She didn't want to betray her father's confidence, but presumably Connors was already aware of what *really* happened and just wanted to know what Jack had experienced. "He believes that you were a man named Peterson and that he killed you in the jungle outside of a place called Nha Trang," she said simply.

Connors nodded his head, but didn't reply, so Sydney continued. "What really happened? Why has my father been living with thirty-five years of guilt over this?"

"Sydney, will you permit me to show you something?" Connors asked. Without waiting for an answer, he stood and began unbuttoning his blue silk shirt, which was immaculate in spite of almost a solid day of traveling.

"Mr. Connors, people will talk," Sydney said jokingly. She was trying to make light of the situation, but it really *was* a strange and uncomfortable moment.

He pulled open his shirt, exposing his chest. Sydney noted that her earlier impression—that in spite of appearances, he was a powerfully built man—was correct. He was well-muscled and far from the sedentary type that his dandified persona and clothing implied. She also noted that he had two thick, raised scars that crisscrossed above his heart. The scars appeared to be many years old, but were no less horrifying for it.

"I *was* Peterson. And for all intents and purposes,

your father *did* kill me in the jungle outside Nha Trang," Connors said quietly while buttoning his shirt.

He was silent for a moment as he finished restoring his clothes to their usual state of perfection, then he sat back down and stared at his own reflection in the darkened window. When he spoke again, it was in a softer voice, almost entirely devoid of his usual theatrics.

"I liked your father," he said. "I admired him greatly. He was a man of almost unbelievable physical and mental strength, yet obviously capable of great compassion as well. When the mission—the experiment, I should say—fell apart, his first thought was for the safety of his men, for those poor boys."

Connors's composure faltered a little, and Sydney could see a tear slip down his face, reflected in the window. "You mean Martin and Lewis?" she asked.

"Yes, those were their names. Martin and Lewis. They were good boys, so devoted to each other. The other man, the mercenary, Hutchins, was a horrible, violent sociopath. Choosing him for the experiment was a mistake that I believe led directly to the violence that followed." Connors pulled a blue silk handkerchief from his pocket and dabbed at his eyes. "Forgive me," he said, turning back to Sydney. "Sometimes I feel like a part of me, and probably a part of your father, never left that jungle."

Seeing that he had recovered a bit, Sydney urged him to continue. "You chose the men for the experiment?" she asked.

"Yes, the entire operation, from start to bloody finish, was my project, my responsibility. I chose your father to lead the mission into the jungle, even though he'd barely been in the CIA a year at that point. I think he was truly excited to be given command of an operation, although he never showed it." Connors fingered the scars through his shirt as he spoke and Sydney could see in his eyes that in his mind he was very far away, reliving the horror of that night. "Everything was supposed to work together, every element perfectly balanced: the physical and mental stresses of the mission, the combination of personalities and experience, and the drug that I administered to those four men. But something was off, a miscalculation was made, and everything went wrong. Your father and I bear the scars of that night. We always will. The others . . . weren't so fortunate."

"What was the point of the experiment?" Sydney

had to ask. "What were you trying to learn?"

He hung his head in shame. "It was the usual nonsense. Can lifelong best friends be chemically induced to turn on each other? Can a battle-hardened soldier be driven into a state of hysterical fear? Can the most rational and calculating of men be reduced to the level of an unthinking beast? I thought that I could control the severity of the reactions. Obviously, I was mistaken."

Sydney gave him a moment to compose himself before asking her next question. "So, after my father attacked you, how was it that you managed to survive out there?"

"Miraculously, I would have to say," Connors replied, and then continued in a quieter voice. "It was touch and go for a while. When we found the first body, and it was apparent that something had gone wrong with the experiment, I triggered a radio beacon that was in my possession, calling for an extraction team. They found me on the verge of death. Your father's blows had missed my heart by the narrowest of margins, but I had lost a great deal of blood. I recuperated in Saigon for a few weeks and then was flown to Washington. All things considered, I would say that I got off lightly. Your father was in even worse shape when they finally found him."

"You never tried to contact him?"

"I considered it, but decided that he would be more satisfied believing that he had killed the man responsible for that slaughter. Later on, I learned that he never suspected that I—that Peterson—was the guilty one at all. He believed that there were other, unseen parties in the jungle with us. He spent years trying to find out who had been running the experiment, who was the cause of all that bloodshed. He got as far as learning that it was someone known as the Ghost, but no further. Jack never learned that Peterson and the Ghost were one and the same person. I buried the alias and let your father and the rest of the world believe that Peterson died in that jungle. It was only yesterday—when Arvin introduced the Ghost, and Jack saw *my* face—that he finally put all the pieces together. I have always known that someday I would have to come forward and take responsibility for what I did out there, but, in retrospect, I probably could have handled it better."

"And that's why you stopped conducting field experiments and removed yourself from the process?" Sydney asked. She believed that Connors was truly repentant, but couldn't resist hammering away at him a little bit. "Tell me . . . was it because those men died, or was it because you were almost killed yourself?"

"To my great shame," he answered, "it was the latter. And, to my even greater shame, Nha Trang was *not* the straw that broke the proverbial camel's back. Typically of so many men in my . . . profession . . . I let my thirst for knowledge trump any ethical considerations that may have arisen. The assignments became more practical, less experimental, in nature, and I ceased putting myself in harm's way. But I continued with my field work for many years—more than I care to think about."

"Is that why you needed the partner? So you could avoid putting yourself in harm's way?"

Again he turned and faced the window, unable to hold Sydney's gaze. "Yes, the man who truly was the Ghost, God rest his soul."

"What was he like?" Sydney asked, realizing that Connors would probably never reveal the dead man's identity.

"He was a bit like your father, actually. He was enormously capable, a good man, but not afraid to get his hands dirty if the situation called for it. I miss him, and his friendship, a great deal."

Realizing that Connors had most likely shared all that he was willing to reveal in regards to his partner, Sydney switched gears. "You said that the assignments became more practical. What does that mean?"

"I—or, I should say, we—began putting the results of my research into effect. The operations were easier to live with, the results easier to stomach, once we were applying them to an enemy instead of tinkering with the heads of our own men. We drove foreign agents insane. For instance, we made an Eastern European dictator believe that it was the ghost of his dead mother feeding him bad military advice—very Shakespearean, that particular job. We caused mass hysteria and rioting in the far-flung reaches of the globe. . . . We even toppled an entire South American government by dosing the wine at a state banquet. Our failures were few, and our successes were spectacular. Our reputation—the Ghost's reputation—grew quickly . . . sometimes the mere mention of the name was enough to spread fear through the ranks of our enemies." Connors smiled, but Sydney could see that the things he was talking about weighed heavily on him. "These were the missions that your Mr. Flinkman finds so fascinating. It was a period of my career that only lasted a few years, but they were very productive years."

"And then your partner died?" Sydney asked.

He took a deep breath before nodding his head and answering. "That's right. After he passed away, I tried to continue with our work on my own. I took an assignment in Yugoslavia. Belgrade, to be exact. And it turned into a nightmare. It was like Nha Trang, but on a much larger scale. Dozens of people were killed and the whole incident had to be covered up and made to look like a bomb had accidentally exploded. If my partner had been there, none of it would have happened. But I *was* there when it happened, and, even though the victims were enemies of the United States—members of some terrorist group or another—I was repulsed by what I saw . . . by what I caused. That was the end of intelligence work for me. I continued with my research, but the focus changed." He shook his head sadly. "Sydney, I know that I can't erase the things that I did, but I hope that I can at least begin to make up for them." He laughed bitterly.

"I've become very much karma-oriented in my old age."

The train rumbled on through the Swiss night, gently rocking the passengers to sleep. The only compartment light that still blazed was in the middle of the third car back from the engine. Anyone looking in that window as the train passed would have seen a troubled young woman, wondering if she was being set up . . . and a tormented old man, wrestling with a past full of demons.

CHAPTER 14

ARENA RAMIREZ, MEXICO CITY

The Arena Ramirez sat in the middle of an industrial wasteland to the east of Benito Juarez International Airport. It was a neighborhood of abandoned warehouses, homeless encampments, and junkyards. The streets were sparsely populated, and you could pretty much count on the fact that the people who *were* around were up to no good.

For years, the owners of the arena had struggled, attempting to convince audiences to venture into a neighborhood that they normally avoided, with a mix of *lucha libre* wrestling, hip-hop concerts, and auto shows. They had limited success at first, but it didn't last long. There was no shortage of other, more attractive venues in Mexico City, and the audiences soon dwindled to a mere handful. Two years ago, the arena's gates had been padlocked and the building had sat empty in the center of its litter-strewn parking lot until just this week. Recently, money had changed hands, keys had been acquired, and the Arena Ramirez was once again hosting an event.

For the past few days, anyone keeping an eye on the arena would have been surprised by the amount of activity going on in and around the building. Generator trucks and a large cleaning crew had been followed a day later by a steady stream of high-end motor homes and ominously blacked out vans. An observer might think that there was some kind of recreational vehicle show coming up, if not for the complete lack of advertising . . . and the midnight arrival of a good number of futuristic-looking, armored assault vehicles.

Now, on this sunny spring morning, an astounding transformation had taken place at the Arena Ramirez. From the outside, it was still an abandoned sports arena with a cracked and overgrown parking lot that hadn't been used in months. Inside, it was host to the most stunning array of high-tech weaponry in the world. It was six a.m., and the Leuba Arms Market was open for business.

Outside Marta Mendoza's hotel, Dixon and Nadia were waiting for their ride. Connors had informed them that special cars brought the customers to and from the Leuba and that they were to flash the daggers to the driver once he approached them. They had only been waiting for a few seconds when a black Towncar entered the hotel's circular drive and came to a smooth stop at the curb in front of the APO agents. The uniformed driver hopped out and rushed around the front of the car to greet them.

"Ms. Mendoza?" he inquired of Nadia. She nodded and showed him the dagger cupped in her palm. After a cursory glance at the dagger that Dixon was wearing on a chain around his neck, the driver bowed slightly and opened the back door of the Towncar. Once they were inside, he got back in the driver's seat and started out on his circuitous route to the Arena Ramirez.

Nadia and Dixon were perfectly aware of their destination, but the real Marta Mendoza and bodyguard would have had no idea where they were headed at this point. The operators of the Leuba prided themselves on taking good care of their guests, but they still had to take certain security precautions. Guests were informed of the date of the market and what city it would be held in. They were always met at their hotels and shuttled back and forth to the actual site. Once they arrived at the market, they would be thoroughly searched; no weapons or communication devices were allowed inside. Connors had forewarned the team of this and they were going in unarmed and without the benefit of comms.

The plan was to identify the man who was offering January for sale, secure him, and then call in a raid on the market. They knew from Connors's intel that they were looking for a man named Lanchester, a small-time dealer of chemical weapons who had only recently earned a first-time seller's spot at the Leuba. Beyond that, they were flying blind.

A combined strike team of CIA agents and Mexican Intelligence had been assembled in the early morning hours and was currently maintaining position a dozen blocks from the arena. The Leuba Market was notorious for having moles and paid informants in many of the world's intelligence and police agencies, so the team had been assembled at the last minute and had yet to be informed of their target.

Once Lanchester had been identified and secured, Dixon was to trigger a signal from a transmitter concealed in the heel of his boot that would call in the raid.

The transmitter was a marvel of engineering, courtesy of Marshall Flinkman. It was composed almost entirely of plastics and organic materials that would not register on a metal detector, and was powered by a chemical reaction that would be set off by mixing two substances together. Dixon was pretty sure he remembered that nitric acid was one of the two, but the other had been buried in a torrent of Marshall-speak. What he *did* remember was how to set the thing off. He was to remove the device from the compartment in his pivoting boot heel and stomp on it—simple as that. The resulting chemical reaction would power a burst transmission that would be received by the strike team that was monitoring the appropriate frequency. The only drawback, according to Marshall, was a slight rotten egg smell that would be released by the combined chemicals. The whole thing sounded pretty sketchy to Dixon, but he had learned over the years to trust Marshall's op-tech, no matter how dubious it might seem on the surface.

The Towncar arrived at the open gates of the arena parking lot and immediately proceeded around to the back side of the building. The driver pulled up to the curb in front of the arena entrance, and Nadia and Dixon were helped from the car by tuxedoed attendants. Their driver assured them that he would be waiting to take them back to the hotel, and then pulled away.

As they made their way up an immaculate red carpet to the doors of the arena, a wheezing, green and white Beetle pulled up and Weiss and Vaughn were unceremoniously deposited on the curb. Dixon was careful not to make eye contact with his fellow agents, but he couldn't help but smile to himself. *Nice car. I guess a Latin American cocaine princess and her bodyguard still outrank a couple of racist bikers,* he thought.

Nadia and Dixon entered through the doors and

into the arena lobby, where they were offered drinks by two beautiful women carrying trays of Bloody Marys and mimosas. They declined the beverages and made their way to the check-in table that waited just outside the walkway that led to the arena floor.

While they waited for two well-known African revolutionaries, clad head-to-toe in camouflage, to present their daggers to the attendant, Nadia took the opportunity to whisper in Dixon's ear. "I really wish I had a picture of the four of us. Sydney will never believe me."

"I was just thinking the same thing," he laughed, and glanced over his shoulder at Vaughn and Weiss.

The four of them really did make quite a sight. Nadia was clad in skintight black leather pants and a tank top that wasn't leaving a lot to the imagination. She was sporting a pair of lace-up boots, courtesy of Marta Mendoza, and was dripping with silver necklaces and bracelets. She was pretty certain that she had never in her life worn as much eyeliner as she currently had on.

Dixon was far and away the most conservatively dressed of the group, although his silk shirt, which was open nearly to the waist, was not his first choice. He had opted for a black turtleneck, but Nadia and the others had badgered him until he agreed to adopt a close approximation of Günther's signature style. His protestations that anyone who knew how Günther dressed would surely know enough to know that *he* wasn't Günther fell on deaf ears. The others had insisted that, if they were going to have to embarrass themselves, he should suffer the same fate . . . although they did allow him to skip the cologne. Dixon was remarkably uncomfortable in most respects, but he had to admit he had grown somewhat fond of the silver chain and dagger around his neck.

It was Vaughn and Weiss who had performed the most striking transformations. Their look was perfect: the denim, the chains, the leather. They both were sporting realistic-looking jailhouse tattoos, courtesy of Nadia and a permanent marker, and Weiss had even painted his fingernails black. Crosses dangled from their earlobes and skull rings adorned their fingers. The distinctive golden lightning-bolt-and-book logo of the Brotherhood of the Shining Night adorned the back of their vests. They were magnificent.

"I'm still not sure about the chaps," Nadia

whispered to Dixon, referring to a piece of wardrobe that Weiss had appropriated from Big Jerk.

"At least he's wearing pants underneath," Dixon deadpanned as the revolutionaries walked off and he and Nadia stepped up to check in.

Nadia stifled a laugh and smiled to the young man sitting at the heavy oak table. "I love the tuxedos," she flirted. "No wonder my father never brought me here." She flashed a ten-thousand-watt smile and presented her dagger for inspection. "Marta Mendoza. And you are . . . ?"

Instantly smitten, the young man gulped and stammered out his name. "Ethan . . . Ethan Fabelo, Ms. Mendoza. Welcome to the Leuba."

She blew him a kiss, practically knocking him over backward, and called for Dixon to follow her. "Come along, Günther."

This was a crucial moment. If the young man at the desk balked at Dixon's appearance, the whole plan could fall apart. The APO agents were unarmed and, although they all seemed very nice, the tuxedoed staff appeared to have shoulder holsters beneath their immaculately tailored jackets.

Dixon held out his dagger for Ethan. "Mr. . . . Hathaway?" the young man asked.

Cool as a cucumber, Dixon lifted an eyebrow and smiled slightly. "Is there a problem?" he asked.

"No . . . I just wasn't expecting . . . ," Ethan sputtered. He looked over at Nadia, who was scowling with impatience. "I wasn't expecting . . . anything," he finished lamely. "Sorry for the delay."

"No problem." Dixon let the kid off the hook with a smile and proceeded with Nadia through the short tunnel that led beneath the arena seating and into the Leuba Arms Market proper.

The market had been founded in the late sixties by Eugene Leuba, the colorful son of a once-powerful arms smuggling family that had fallen on hard times. Eugene was a notorious playboy with a taste for excess, and he ran the market accordingly. The international criminal community had responded to the flamboyant event with enthusiasm, and the family's fortunes had seen a dramatic turnaround. Eugene had passed on in the early eighties, but his son, Eugene II, had kept the market, and the family, thriving.

The market was held twice a year for one day only. It was only open for six hours, and although sellers of everything—save for chemical and biological weapons—were encouraged to have samples of their wares on display, no weapons were to change hands at the market itself. Deals were struck and arrangements for delivery were made. Any seller violating these rules would be dealt with severely by the Leuba family and most likely never seen again.

Once they passed through the tunnel and arrived on the arena floor, Dixon and Nadia were dazzled by what they saw. Dixon whistled and then shook his head in amazement. "This is incredible," he said, and Nadia seconded that opinion with a nod of her head.

The entire floor of the arena had been transformed into a decadent playground for unscrupulous adults. There were maybe two dozen motor homes and half as many assault vehicles parked on the floor, with elaborate displays of weaponry in front of all of them. Techno music was being pumped into the space, and dancers in bikinis, or even less, were gyrating on top of the tanks and RVs. Scantily clad waitresses roamed the floor, offering the customers drinks—and substances of a less legal nature—while beautiful women in evening gowns displayed the firepower that was being offered for sale. There were fire-eaters and contortionists and jugglers roaming the crowd, while a troupe of gymnasts wearing only body paint performed an erotic aerial act above the revelers' heads.

"Wow . . . dinner *and* a show," Dixon murmured appreciatively.

Nadia was astounded. "I can't believe these people have the stamina for this kind of thing at six in the morning. It boggles the mind," she remarked, using an expression that Weiss had just recently taught her.

The weapons on display were mind-boggling in their own right. There was the expected array of machine pistols, assault rifles, grenade launchers, and armor-piercing ammunition, all available in massive quantities; but there were also items of a more esoteric nature. Shoulder-fired missiles, small rockets that could be retrofitted to deliver a chemical payload, and sonic weapons that were capable of disabling an entire crowd in seconds were all available . . . for the right price. The assault vehicles—all next-generation stuff that looked straight out of a science-fiction movie—were also on the auction block. Many of the vendors had video monitors set up, showing their products in action. A few even had makeshift firing ranges set up and the already deafening music was occasionally drowned out by a volley of machine gun fire. Most of the actual deal making took place within the confines of the luxurious motor homes that were rented for the occasion.

Nadia was amused to note a number of go-go boys mixed in with the writhing bikini girls. It was refreshing that the market offered a little something for everyone, no matter what their taste, but it was the fact that the male dancers were wearing chaps that brought the smile to her face. She made a mental note to tease Eric about his up-to-the-minute fashion sense.

Because they were working without comms, Dixon and Nadia waited until they had seen Vaughn and Weiss enter the arena floor before moving deeper into the market. They would walk the floor, trying to ascertain who Lanchester was, while maintaining visual contact with their fellow agents. One of the unfortunate aspects of Vaughn and Weiss's alias, beyond the chaps, was that they most likely wouldn't be seen chatting with Nadia and Dixon—the Brotherhood would hardly approve.

* * *

The vendors and their vehicles were laid out in rows, like the streets of a small, heavily-armed town. As they worked their way through the market, keeping Nadia and Dixon in sight, Vaughn and Weiss did their best to look like a pair of surly racists. It wasn't easy, especially since Weiss was practically bubbling over with enthusiasm. "This is amazing," he said. "Absolutely amazing. It's like the greatest boat show in history. Have you ever been to a boat show? It's just like this, only with boats instead of weapons. Boat shows are great. Hello, ladies."

Weiss was addressing a pair of bikini-clad beauties who were enthusiastically dancing on either side of a video monitor displaying spectacular footage of a shoulder-fired rocket streaking through the sky and destroying an enormous yacht anchored off of what appeared to be the coast of Greece.

"Hi, guys. I'm Kim," said the bubbly brunette.

"I'm Lindsey," murmured the bashful blonde.

"Are you guys looking to beef up your arsenal?" Kim asked dancing all the while.

"I'm not even sure how to answer that," Weiss replied, as Vaughn grabbed his arm and dragged him away. "You see what I'm saying?" he asked Vaughn. "Greatest boat show of all time."

Vaughn was less interested in gyrating spokesmodels and more interested in the firepower that was being offered wholesale to a cross section of the world's most dangerous criminals. "Look at this stuff," he said, cutting off Weiss's ode to boat shows. "*We* don't even have access to half of this stuff. Why is it that every two-bit drug lord and dictator can get their hands on these things, while we have to fill out half a dozen forms just to requisition a new holster? What is that about?"

Weiss had seen his friend like this before and knew that there was no sense in trying to lighten the mood with a joke. He clapped Vaughn on the shoulder and did his best to defuse the situation. "Don't worry," he said. "After today, they won't be selling so much as a slingshot." Vaughn just grunted, and they continued their search for the chemical weapons dealer who was peddling January.

It quickly became apparent that the market, like any town, had neighborhoods . . . and that some neighborhoods were more desirable than others. The displays toward the center of the floor were more elaborate and offered a higher quality product. There *were* dealers hawking chemical and biological weapons in some of these larger displays—ricin, sarin, and VX gas, all of which were being offered in quantities that terrified the APO team—but Connors had made it clear that the man they were looking for was a small fish who would most likely be peddling things that the big guys wouldn't touch. If Lanchester was anywhere, he was going to be on the outskirts. The team made their way through the "streets," trying to identify someone who looked like they might fit the description of a small-time chemical weapons dealer named Lanchester.

"Hey there, big guy. My name's Lanchester, Billy Lanchester, and if it's chemical weapons you're looking for, you've come to the right place. I'm having a one-day-only special on anthrax."

Well, that was easy, Nadia thought. The weasel-faced man with lank, greasy hair was planted in front of a light brown panel truck and addressed Dixon in a nasal voice that was like fingernails on a chalkboard. He stood next to a crudely painted sign on an easel that also proclaimed his name and specialty, and was wearing a velour tracksuit the exact same color as his truck. "Actually," Nadia said, "it's me you should be addressing. And chemical weapons are just the sort of thing that I *am* looking for."

Lanchester smoothed his hair down with one hand, and then offered Nadia a deep bow. Before she could pull away, he grabbed her right arm and planted a wetter-than-necessary kiss on the back of her hand. "Billy Lanchester, procurer of exotic chemical weapons, at your disposal."

He straightened up and leered at Nadia through bloodshot eyes. "And what is it that I can offer you, my pet?"

Nadia swallowed her revulsion and batted her eyes at Lanchester. "Is there someplace we can talk? I have a delicate matter to attend to and"—she indicated Weiss and Vaughn loitering nearby—"it's a little too public out here for my taste."

"Certainly, my angel, we can talk in the back of my truck. Will your"—he fished for some clue to Dixon's role—"bodyguard . . . be accompanying us?"

"Of course," she replied quickly, not wanting to be alone with this creep for even a second. "Where I go, he goes."

Lanchester was disappointed and made no effort to hide it. "Right this way then." He gestured toward the rear doors of the truck.

"Hey, buddy," Weiss called out. "Can we talk to you about your products?"

Lanchester, thrilled by the sudden attention—his first potential patrons of the day, in fact—attempted to sound businesslike. "I'm with a customer right now, but if you would like to step around back, my associate can show you some video of our field tests and I will be with you shortly."

The entire team took note of Lanchester's mention of an unseen associate. They were on the far edge of the arena floor, behind the bigger displays, and the only other vendor in sight was a man in front of a small motor home with a paltry-looking selection of machine guns and a World War II vintage bazooka. The man was sitting in a folding lawn chair and appeared to be asleep. Other than that, their little corner of the market was deserted. Apparently small-timers didn't warrant dancers and cocktail waitresses.

Nadia and Dixon stepped up into the back of the truck with Lanchester while Vaughn and Weiss walked around to the back to watch videos with the associate.

The associate was sitting on a green plastic lawn chair that threatened to collapse beneath his bulk. He was an enormous man, close to seven feet tall, and had arms and legs like tree trunks. He was wearing a tracksuit that matched Lanchester's, but didn't even come close to fitting him properly. There was an equally ill-fitting toupee on his head and incongruous red tennis shoes on his feet. But his most striking feature, other than his size, was the deep, crimson scar that ran from ear to ear across his throat. Clearly someone had tried to send this giant of a man to meet his maker at some point . . . and had failed in the attempt.

When he saw Weiss and Vaughn, the giant hit stop and then rewind on a remote control and struggled to his feet, motioning for the two men to take a seat. There were a handful of plastic chairs on an artificial lawn behind Lanchester's truck, arranged in a semicircle around a TV monitor. There was also a cooler of beer sitting nearby. Weiss struggled to keep from laughing at the absurdity of the situation.

They sat down in two of the chairs and declined the giant's silent offer of beer. Once they were seated comfortably, the giant stood behind them and gestured for them to watch the TV before hitting a button on the remote. The image flickered and rolled a few times, and then began to play.

Lanchester climbed into the truck behind Nadia and Dixon, shutting the doors once he was inside. The back of the vehicle was cluttered with boxes and various engine parts, and everything seemed to be coated in a combination of grease and dust. Lanchester moved a couple of boxes to the floor, revealing an uncomfortable-looking wooden bench, and gestured for Nadia and Dixon to have a seat. When they were situated, he perched himself on a wooden crate labeled "Flammable" and clapped his hands twice as if calling a meeting to order.

"And what is it that I can offer such a beautiful lady?" he asked in his unappealing voice.

"My name is Marta Mendoza," Nadia began. "Perhaps you have heard of me? Or, rather, my father? No? It's doesn't matter. What *does* matter is the fact that my father was murdered by treacherous pigs, and now it is time for them to pay."

Dixon didn't say a word, but he was impressed with the way Nadia handled their oily host. She knew instinctively how to push this guy's buttons. Lanchester was definitely the type to be drawn to crazy—the crazier the better—and Nadia laid it on thick and fast.

"I don't just want to kill them. If a bullet in the head would suffice, I would have had it done months ago. No . . . death is not enough for these jackals. I want to take their souls. I want them to watch their wives and children and everyone that they've ever loved driven mad before their eyes. I want to destroy everyone and everything that they have ever held dear. And I want you to help me do it."

Lanchester was hooked. If he were a religious man, he would have thanked the gods for sending him this dark, scary angel. His face cracked into a grotesque smile and he leaned forward and took Nadia's hands as he spoke. "My dear, you have found your man. And it would be an honor and a privilege to assist you in your quest for vengeance."

Nadia held her breath and leaned in close to Lanchester, who was practically salivating. "So, what can you offer me? How are we going to do this?"

Aroused by Nadia's use of the word *we*, Lanchester leaped to his feet and began sorting through a stack of boxes. "Let me show you something exciting," he said. "I could've sworn that I left it . . . oh yes, here it is."

He pulled a battered leather briefcase, held together with duct tape, out from under the bench where Dixon and Nadia were sitting, sat back down on his crate, and placed the case on his thighs. He popped open the rusty latches and removed a glass vial capped with a rubber stopper and half filled with a clear liquid. "This is exactly what *we* need. It is liquid madness. I call it January," he said, taking credit for Connors's name.

Dixon and Nadia had a brief second of concerned eye contact. One of the cardinal rules of the Leuba Arms Market was that dealers of chemical or biological weapons were not, under any circumstances, to have samples of their products on site. It was only grudgingly, after the death of Eugene I, that the Leuba family bowed to pressure from their clients and allowed such things to be sold at the market at all. The fact that Lanchester had a sample of January on hand meant that they would have to proceed with extreme caution. Taking Lanchester down wasn't going to be a problem—he would crumple like a sheet of paper—but they couldn't risk the accidental release of the chemical, and there was no telling what else he might have lying around.

"May I ask why you call it January?" Nadia asked, hoping that Lanchester would set the vial aside so that she and Dixon could move in on him.

"Well . . . because . . . ," Lanchester stammered, obviously unprepared for the question. He was spared further embarrassment by an enormous crash as something slammed into the outside wall of the truck. "What the hell was that?" he asked, setting down the briefcase and the vial of January.

As Lanchester rose to his feet, intent on finding out what the disturbance was, Dixon gave Nadia an almost imperceptible nod and then launched himself at the sleazy purveyor of chemical weapons. He struck Lanchester square in the back and propelled him forward, into the closed door of the truck. Lanchester's head made contact with the metal door with a satisfying thump, knocking him unconscious. Dixon dropped him on the floor of the truck in a heap. "Keep an eye on him," he said to Nadia.

As Nadia got to work, refastening Lanchester's sample case and checking the truck for any further evidence of January, Dixon opened the back door to check on Vaughn and Weiss.

Vaughn didn't even last five minutes once the giant started the video tape. The silent, black-and-white image on the monitor was very low quality, but it was clear enough.

The first scene was of a young man, twenty years old at most, wearing torn, dirty clothes and looking in desperate need of a shower, a shave, and a meal. If Vaughn had to guess, he would have pegged the young man as a runaway. He was handcuffed, and one of his legs was shackled to what appeared to be a concrete park bench. The bench was sitting in the middle of an empty warehouse and the young man appeared to be yelling for help. The shadow of the cameraman was visible in the shot, and its size indicated that it could only be made by their friend the giant.

Someone approached the young man from behind the camera and squirted him in the face with a cheap, plastic squirt gun. When he turned around and started back toward the camera, Vaughn and Weiss recognized the man with the squirt gun as Lanchester.

After a few seconds, the young man began to convulse violently. His body jerked back and forth while he clawed at his own face with his cuffed hands. Behind Vaughn and Weiss, the eerily silent giant broke out with a huge smile and began to applaud. When the man on the screen began to vomit blood, Vaughn closed his eyes, steeling his nerves for what he had to do next.

There was no way for Vaughn to communicate his intentions to Weiss. The giant was standing right behind them and, unless he was deaf as well as mute, he couldn't help but overhear anything that they said. Vaughn was just going to have to make a move and trust that Weiss was ready. It was definitely going to take both of them to subdue the giant . . . particularly since they had to do it without alerting anyone else in the arena.

Vaughn took a deep breath and then stood up, driving the chair backward with his legs and into the giant's groin. He immediately wheeled around and unleashed a jab into the big man's horribly scarred throat, hoping to disable him quickly. The giant looked more surprised than injured and swatted at Vaughn with one huge palm, knocking him to the ground.

Weiss was instantly on his feet and swinging. Two quick blows to the giant's midsection had no discernible effect. A swift kick to the shin was met with a grunt. The giant pushed Weiss away with both hands, sending him toppling backward over one of the lawn chairs.

Vaughn was back on his feet and ready for more. The giant lumbered toward him and Vaughn responded with a jumping spin kick that brought his foot into solid contact with the behemoth's jaw. Any other man would have crumpled, but the giant didn't even slow his forward motion. He caught Vaughn's leading foot in one enormous paw and jerked upward, completely upending the smaller man. The giant then grabbed the back of Vaughn's denim vest with the other hand and, without even the slightest hint of effort, lifted Vaughn above his head and slammed him full force into the side of the truck.

A length of silver chain whistled through the air and opened a deep cut on the big man's left cheek. He let go of Vaughn, who dropped to the ground with a groan, and turned to face Weiss, who had removed one of the chains from his jacket and was spinning it with one hand. "Come on, Godzilla," Weiss taunted. "Come and get it."

The giant rushed forward surprisingly quickly and got inside Weiss's reach. The chain came down ineffectually on the giant's back as he wrapped his arms around Weiss and lifted him off his feet.

Dixon stepped out of the back of the truck just in time to see the giant squeezing the air out of a squirming Weiss. The strange sight caught him off guard for a fraction of a second, but he recovered quickly and rushed to his friend's assistance. He put his shoulder down and plowed into the giant's side at full speed, pushing him over an upturned chair. Weiss, Dixon, and their huge opponent tumbled to the ground. The giant's grip was broken, and a grateful Weiss rolled away, gasping for air.

As Dixon jumped to his feet and rained a series of blows on the still-upended giant, Vaughn pulled himself upright and immediately began searching for something to use as a weapon. His eyes lit on the monitor.

The giant managed to roll over and knock Dixon's feet out from underneath him with a sweep of his arm. Dixon didn't miss a beat. He hammered at the giant's legs with his heels then quickly crab-walked backward, out of reach. The giant had just struggled to his knees when Vaughn brought the TV monitor down on top of his head with as much force as he could muster.

The giant teetered back and forth for a second and then collapsed face down on the arena floor. Weiss had regained his breath enough to rise to his feet, and the three APO agents looked at each other in disbelief. Their moment of shared incredulity was cut short by the door of the truck opening and a cowed Lanchester stepping out, followed closely by Nadia, who had his arm twisted behind his back in what looked to be an incredibly uncomfortable position.

"What happened to you guys?" Nadia inquired, marveling at her comrades' bruised and battered appearance.

Weiss, not quite recovered enough to speak, jerked his thumb in the direction of the mammoth, unconscious body a few feet away and watched Nadia's eyes go wide with amazement.

"That would explain it," she muttered. Lanchester laughed and earned himself a sharp, painful twist of the arm.

"Let's get out of here," Vaughn said.

As Dixon crossed to the back of the truck and grabbed Lanchester's briefcase, Nadia laid down the law to her captive. "We're walking out of here . . . together. If you so much as blink at anyone on the way, I promise you I'll snap your skinny arm like a twig. You got it?"

Lanchester nodded and the five of them walked out from behind the truck. The dealer next door was still snoozing in his chair, completely unaware of anything amiss. There was still no one else in sight.

Vaughn was in the lead, followed by Nadia and Lanchester, with Weiss and Dixon bringing up the rear. The only exit from the market was all the way across the arena floor, through the same door that they came in. Instead of cutting through the crowded center, Vaughn was leading them around the outer edge of the floor.

As they started walking, Weiss wrinkled his

nose and waved his hand in front of his face. "Whoa," he said to Dixon. "What did you have for breakfast?"

Dixon was about to ask Weiss what he was talking about when he caught the distinct, sulfurous whiff of rotten eggs. He lifted his left foot and noted that his boot heel was slightly askew and some kind of viscous liquid was dripping from the compartment inside. "We need to move. Quickly," he said.

The group picked up the pace, trying to hurry without drawing unwanted attention. "What's up?" Vaughn asked.

"During the fight the beacon trigger got smashed . . . probably when I tried to kick that man-mountain. They'll be raiding this place any minute and we're going to be trapped in the middle."

"Okay," Vaughn replied, laying on more speed. "Let's get to the door."

They skirted the edge of the market, making good time without being conspicuous, and were almost to the exit when their attention was drawn by a volley of high-pitched screams. Whipping around to see the source of the disturbance, they were amazed to see the apparently unstoppable giant, blood streaming from his scalp, charging through the gap between two motor homes and bearing down on them with silent fury. He had pushed over a large display of high-tech weaponry and sent Kim and Lindsey—Weiss's bikini-clad friends and the source of the screaming—scattering in his wake.

Vaughn yelled for Nadia and Dixon to keep moving. "Go! Get Lanchester and the sample out of here," he called as he and Weiss turned to face their nemesis. Lanchester tried to take advantage of the moment and yell for help but Nadia was ready for him. As soon as he opened his mouth, she yanked up and back on his arm, dislocating his shoulder with a sickening pop.

"Move," she commanded, and propelled him toward the exit.

Weiss dodged the giant's charge, slipping out of reach at the last second, but Vaughn wasn't so lucky. The huge man hit Vaughn full force, knocking him to the ground. Vaughn landed on his side and felt something give way inside his chest. He had broken ribs before and immediately recognized the pain and inability to draw more than the shallowest of breaths. He groaned and attempted to scramble away from the action as Weiss faced off with the giant.

Not wanting a replay of his earlier encounter, Weiss looked around for something—anything—that would give him some kind of advantage against his enormous foe.

"Hey, biker guy!" Weiss spun around to see Lindsey, the blond spokesmodel, holding up what looked like a short, fat shotgun. "It's loaded," she called, and tossed the weapon to him with a wink. Weiss caught the grenade launcher perfectly and spun around to face the giant.

The big man was angry, but he wasn't stupid. As soon as he saw the grenade launcher in Weiss's hands, he turned and ran, as fast as a moving mountain could run. Weiss called a heartfelt "Thank you, Lindsey" over his shoulder as he helped Vaughn to his feet and they limped their way to the exit.

Their timing was impeccable. As they emerged into the bright Mexico City sunlight, half a dozen large vehicles were screeching to a halt in front of the arena and disgorging squads of heavily armed men. Dixon waved them over to an armored transport that had been first on the scene.

"You think we should warn them about the big guy?" Weiss asked as the raid commenced.

"They'd never believe us," Vaughn managed to wheeze before collapsing to the ground.

CHAPTER 15

SWITZERLAND

Sometime in the hour just before dawn, the train stopped in the small mountain village of Brannen. A few sleepy-eyed passengers stepped down from the train, having reached the end of their journey, only to be replaced by eager travelers just starting out. Sydney had been napping fitfully for the past few hours but was jolted awake by the squeal of the brakes as the train came to a halt.

A bright-eyed American couple in their late thirties boarded the train and joined Sydney and Connors in their compartment for the final leg of the trip to Taviston. Connors slipped across to share the bench with a sleepy Sydney while the couple sat down opposite and introduced themselves as Christopher and May Harrington.

As Sydney and Connors exchanged pleasantries with the couple, it was revealed that they were all traveling to the same destination. May's grandmother, apparently the widow of a fabulously wealthy Texas oil tycoon, had been a resident of the Devereaux for the past nine months, and the couple was on the way to pay her a visit after doing a little Swiss sightseeing.

"Grandma Genevieve insisted that we make a vacation out of it. . . . It's our first time in Europe. She's a wonderful woman," said Christopher.

"Are you . . . visiting someone at the clinic?" May asked delicately, afraid of the answer she might get. Connors turned on the charm and broke the bad news in his own inimitable fashion.

"I'm afraid, my dear, that I will be taking up residency at the clinic myself. Although I dare say that if Grandma Genevieve is half the charmer that you are, I'm definitely looking forward to my new surroundings."

May smiled, but her eyes betrayed her embarrassment at bringing up such a sensitive subject. "I'm sorry that you're not feeling well," she said.

"Nonsense, Miss May, I feel perfectly fine," he answered, hoping to set her at ease. "It's my doctors who think I must be feeling poorly. I tell them that I'm right as rain, but if they want to keep charging me their ridiculous fees, they have to find something wrong with me. Still . . . if it gives me a chance to rest my bones for a while on the shores of lovely Lake Lucerne, who am I to argue?" He patted Sydney's leg gently. "Besides, I had been promising my daughter a trip to Europe for years. It seemed like the perfect excuse."

"Have you been over before, Ms. Connors?"

It took Sydney a moment to realize that Christopher was addressing her. "Once," she answered a little groggily, "just after college."

Connors came to her aid and filled in the details of Sydney's trip to the couple. "It was one of those wretched backpacking trips: youth hostels, hitchhiking . . . the whole nine yards. I tried to get her to let me pay for a grand tour, but she's every bit as stubborn as I am. She's always refusing to help her old man squander his ill-gotten gains." He gazed at Sydney with remarkably believable affection in his eyes. "I wish that I had even a fraction of her integrity."

Sydney shook the cobwebs from her brain and resigned herself to staying awake for the final hours of their trip. She entered into the conversation and was pleased to find that May and Christopher were a charming and interesting couple. May let slip that they were expecting their first child and they were heartily congratulated by Sydney and her eccentric "father."

Connors seemed to be enjoying himself immensely, playing up the loving father alias and keeping their companions amused, but Sydney thought that he wasn't looking his best. His skin had assumed a grayish pallor and the mischievous twinkle in his eyes had dimmed. She told herself that it was just the effects of the long journey that she was seeing, nothing to worry about, and joined in with his uproarious reminiscence of "Sydney Connors's" eighth birthday party.

". . . and there she stood," he was saying, "covered from head to toe in chocolate cake, not knowing whether to laugh or cry."

"It was *lemon* cake, and I didn't fall. . . . I was tripped," Sydney corrected him.

Connors laughed and followed her lead. "Oh yes, tripped. You were tripped by the mysterious boy in the blue shirt," he said, then addressed May and Christopher. "No such creature ever surfaced, but she still, after all these years, insists that the boy in the blue shirt was the guilty party . . . tripped her for no good reason. Like I said . . . she's a stubborn one."

The mood in the car was warm and comfortable, in spite of the early hour. Sydney found herself reflecting on her father—her *real* father—and his experience with the man that she was sitting next to. It didn't surprise her that Jack had initially been fond of Connors—or Peterson, or whatever his name actually was—when they were on the Nha Trang mission. It seemed to her that there were great similarities between the men, in spite of the outward differences. They were both possessed of penetrating intellects, and they each displayed outward personas that served to mask the depths of their true feelings. And both of them seemed to be capable of committing acts that most people would balk at, without losing their humanity. She was saddened to realize that if things had worked out differently, her father and Connors would most likely have remained friends.

As they approached Taviston, Connors launched into an elaborate story involving a family vacation to the Grand Canyon, a roadside souvenir stand, and a wooden cigar-store Indian that Sydney had befriended. It was a charming, funny story, and Connors effortlessly made it seem like one that he had told for years. When he got to the part where six-year-old Sydney proclaimed, "I just thought he was the quiet type," everyone in the car had a good laugh.

As she laughed, it briefly crossed Sydney's mind that she couldn't have shared too many moments like this with Jack—he wasn't around for much of her childhood—but her thought was cut short by Connors's hearty laughter turning into a painful, violent cough.

It quickly became apparent that this was no ordinary cough. Connors was racked with pain. He broke out in a cold sweat and doubled over with each new lung-tearing spasm. Sydney tried to comfort him, but she wasn't entirely sure how concerned she should be—the cough definitely didn't *seem* like an act, but Connors was nothing if not dedicated to his role playing. For their part, Christopher and May seemed very upset about

Connors's attack and tried to help as best they could. Christopher stood, declaring his intention to go find someone to provide medical attention, but Connors grabbed his wrist and prevented the younger man from leaving.

The coughing finally subsided and Connors waved off Sydney's offer of water. He pulled out his handkerchief to wipe his damp face and forehead. Sydney noted that there were tiny flecks of blood dotting the cloth after Connors brushed it across his lips.

"Please forgive me, everyone," Connors panted once he had regained sufficient breath. "I feel I must have overexerted myself in the past several days. I'm fine now."

He hardly seemed fine to the others in the compartment, but there wasn't time to worry about that. The train was pulling into the station at Taviston and they only had a few moments to gather their belongings and disembark. Connors seemed to be severely weakened by the coughing fit and gladly accepted Sydney's help stepping down from the train to the wooden platform.

The town itself was a picture-perfect Swiss village, but their little party paid no attention to the scenery. They were focusing on Connors and his well-being.

A chauffeured car—a gorgeous black Bentley, Sydney noted—was waiting to take Christopher and May to the clinic. They tried their best to convince Connors and Sydney to ride with them, but the older man insisted that there wouldn't be room for all of them and their luggage. "Besides," he said, "I'd like to sit for a moment and catch my breath. You should run along now and have lunch with your lovely grandmother. We will see you soon."

Sydney also assured the couple that she and her father would be fine and, reluctantly, they took their leave. As the striking black automobile pulled away from the station, Sydney escorted Connors to a nearby bench and sat down beside him. "What the hell was that about?" she demanded.

He smiled reassuringly and patted her hand. "You mean the cough? It's nothing to worry about, Sydney. It's all part of the cover."

"You were coughing up blood," she retorted. "How is that part of our cover?"

"I should have warned you, but once our cozy little cabin was invaded I never got the chance. I took a pill, a little something of my own devising, which is designed to mimic the symptoms that a man in my supposed condition might display. I daresay it mimicked them a bit too well."

"Didn't you test it out first?" an incredulous Sydney asked.

"I have to admit," he replied, "my preparations in the past few weeks were a little rushed and I never got around to that particular task. But don't fear—I shan't be taking it again."

The bracing mountain air seemed to be doing right by Connors; the color had begun to return to his cheeks. But Sydney wasn't taking any chances. "You wait here for a minute. I'll grab a cab and get our luggage sorted out."

He smiled at her, the twinkle returning to his eyes. "What a good daughter I have. If we hurry, we can still catch the luncheon service at the clinic. I've been told that it's spectacular."

CHAPTER 16

The Devereaux Clinic sat on a breathtakingly beautiful hill overlooking the eastern shore of Lake Lucerne. The central building was a renovated hotel, built in the late thirties, that had once been a popular summer spot for the cream of European society. The hotel had fallen on hard times and closed its doors in the late seventies. It sat empty for more than a decade before being purchased and renovated by Connors sometime in the early nineties.

The main building of the clinic was a sprawling

stone and wood structure that resembled a Swiss chalet on steroids. The enormous, peak-roofed central hall, once the lobby of the hotel, featured a reception desk, comfortable leather furniture, and a fireplace bigger than many people's homes. The gigantic windows on the back wall offered the spectacular vista of Lake Lucerne and the mountains beyond, and large panes of glass set into the A-frame roof allowed for natural light and a view of the sky. Two wings spread out on either side of the center, three stories high, with balconies on all sides and gabled roofs and windows. The central section soared a good three stories above the wings.

The only other buildings on the property were a small greenhouse and a good-size barn that had housed a dozen or more horses during the hotel's heyday. Now the barn was empty, save for riding mowers and the other equipment used to maintain the clinic's immaculate lawns and gardens.

After a half-hour drive on potentially treacherous mountain roads, Sydney and Connors passed over an imposing stone bridge that spanned a rocky gorge, and then passed through a densely wooded area that opened up to reveal the clinic perched on the hill above. The entrance to the grounds was marked by two large stone pillars that supported intricate wrought-iron gates. There was a security booth at these gates—the guard waved them through without pause—and a tall, wrought-iron fence surrounded the property, but Connors assured Sydney that these precautions were only in place to prevent any of the less lucid patients from wandering away. "It's definitely not what you would call a high-security facility," he remarked.

As they entered the grounds, Sydney could see the barn to the left of and slightly behind the main building. The structures were separated by beautiful green lawns. The ground sloped off behind the barn, leading to the cliffs above the lake. The greenhouse wasn't visible from the front of the clinic, but Connors said that it was off to the right, past the extravagant gardens that were bordered by well-trimmed hedges. He promised to take her on a tour of the grounds after they ate.

They had made good time from Taviston and arrived at the clinic in time for lunch, which was even better than Connors had implied. After lunch, they checked in at the reception desk and were given keys to adjoining rooms on the second floor of the South Wing. Their cover story had Sydney staying with her father for a few days—just long enough to get him settled.

The receptionist at the desk informed Connors that he had an appointment to meet with his doctor at one. She assured him that his records had arrived from the United States and that this afternoon's meeting was just a meet and greet so that he and his doctor could get acquainted.

Connors thanked her profusely and then led Sydney to the bank of elevators that serviced the South Wing. "I'm glad to see that they're keeping the place in good condition," he whispered as they crossed the lobby.

The rooms were comfortable and furnished with well-preserved Danish Modern pieces that had been the very height of fashion when they were first purchased in the early fifties. Sydney and Connors's rooms were connected by a shared bathroom and by a small wooden balcony that overlooked the front lawns. All in all, she reflected, it would be a lovely place to relax for a while. *Maybe I can get myself checked in after this is all over.*

Connors excused himself in order to shower and change clothes in preparation for his appointment, then joined Sydney in her room. She asked if, for the sake of their cover story, she should accompany Connors to the meeting with the doctor, but he didn't think it would be necessary. "I'm quite familiar with these meetings—they're one of the things that I monitor while looking for potential test subjects. In fact, I imagine that they'll be transmitting my own session to the house in Cifani," he laughed. "Fortunately, I think that I possess the medical knowledge necessary to be able to tell the doctor what he needs to hear."

"You aren't going to take one of those pills again, are you?" Sydney asked. "The doctor doesn't need to actually see you cough up blood, does he?"

"No," he answered with conviction, "I'm sure that the proper answers to his questions, accompanied by the falsified records that I had sent ahead, will be enough to convince the old sawbones."

"I've read it in books, but I don't think I've ever heard anyone actually use the term 'sawbones' before," she laughed.

"Stick with me, kid," he said, affecting the tone of an old vaudeville comic. "There's more where that came from." He checked his appearance in the mirror, and then made his way to the door. "Have a look around the building while I'm gone," he suggested. "I should be back in an hour or so and we can take a walk around the grounds. We'll discuss this evening's entertainment."

Once Connors was gone, Sydney availed herself of a shower and fresh clothes. She had been planning on napping for an hour, but the water revived her and she decided to follow his suggestion.

She rode the elevator down to the lobby and strolled through the mammoth space, making mental note of exits and potential hiding places. There were beautiful glass and wood doors on the front and back side of the center section, and less grand exit doors at the far end of either wing. Carpeted staircases led upward off either side of the lobby, and emergency stairwells were located at both ends of the North and South Wings.

The lobby was about as comfortable as a space that large could be. The furniture was warm and inviting, the fire was constantly maintained at the perfect level, and the rugs that covered the flagstone floors were as soft as they were beautiful. There was a gorgeous grand piano surrounded by couches, and a good-size bar along the south wall. Sydney was amused to note that even at this hour the bar was well patronized—that must have been part of what Connors meant by providing the guests with "as much comfort as humanly possible."

On the ride from Taviston, Connors had gone into more detail about the clinic's guests—and the staff of doctors and nurses that looked after them. He said that they liked to maintain occupancy at slightly less than a hundred—not counting the two dozen or so shadow patients—even though the facility could easily accommodate twice that many. This allowed for a lot more personal attention to be paid to every guest. "We couldn't justify the ridiculous fees we charge if we didn't kiss each and every rosy red behind equally," he had proclaimed grandly.

Most of the staff, including the two world-class chefs that presided over the kitchens, lived at the clinic full-time and occupied the North Wing. The cleaning crews and the kitchen help generally lived in town, but they were always welcome to stay if room was available.

Connors proudly pointed out that they had guests from all over the world—and a staff to match—and Sydney could see that it was true. In the short period that she had been there, she had heard conversations in English, French, German, Russian, and Italian. When they had first arrived, there was a rotund gentleman in a too-small bathing suit angrily complaining in very loud Japanese about the temperature of the water in the pool to the clearly befuddled receptionist. Sydney had considered stepping in to help, but she wasn't sure if speaking fluent Japanese was a believable character trait for Sydney Connors to possess. Fortunately, a Japanese-speaking nurse had arrived on the scene and whisked the angry bather away.

Curious to get a look at the pools—although she hoped to avoid a further look at the angry bather—Sydney flagged down a stern-looking female nurse and asked for directions.

"The pools, sauna, and steam rooms can be reached by taking the South Wing elevators to the basement level," proclaimed the woman, whose nametag declared her to be Nurse Burnett. Sydney thanked her and was turning back toward the elevators when the nurse spoke again. "You're Ms. Connors, aren't you?" Sydney replied that she was, and Nurse Burnett smiled warmly. "Welcome, Ms. Connors. Sydney, isn't it?" Sydney nodded. "Welcome, Sydney. Now you listen to me—I don't want you to worry about a thing. We're going to take very good care of your father. If you need anything while you're here, anything at all, just ask for me—Nurse Burnett. And if you feel like joining us, I hold a little Bible study session every evening in the North Wing meeting hall. Do you have a minute to talk?"

Nurse Burnett was obviously ramping up to a full-blown sermon, so Sydney thanked her again, and managed to extricate herself by asking for directions to the nearest restroom. She waited until the nurse had disappeared from view, and then took the elevators to the basement.

The lower level was almost as impressive as the main floor. There was a half-Olympic-size pool, wet and dry saunas, a large Jacuzzi, and a good number of massage and dressing rooms. A sign on the wall by the pool pointed the way to the dance studio and gymnasium, located under the North Wing. The walls and ceilings were painted a deep blue, and a light mist hung in the warm air. There were tile mosaics, some of them worn and chipped with age, depicting mythological scenes on the walls and the bottom of the crystal-clear pool. The ceilings were very low, and the dark paint gave the entire level the feel of some exotic subterranean grotto. All in all, it was a scene worthy of a Roman emperor.

Even though the mosaics obviously predated Connors's renovations, Sydney noted that the figure depicted in the center of the pool, looking two ways at once, was his old friend Janus. *No wonder he wanted to buy this place,* she thought.

Connors would be done with his meeting soon, so Sydney took the elevator back to the second floor. As she stepped out, she was greeted by the spectacle of a tiny woman—no more than four and a half feet tall, Sydney guessed—clad in a garish flowered sundress, huge sunglasses, and an enormous straw hat. Her neck dripped with strand after strand of beautiful, flawless pearls, and she attempted to enter the elevator before realizing that Sydney was attempting to exit.

"Oh, hello there, I didn't see you." She peered at Sydney over the top of her glasses. "You're the newcomer, aren't you? Who was that handsome man I saw you dining with earlier?"

"That's my father," Sydney replied. "He'll be joining you here for a while. My name's Sydney—Sydney Connors."

The old lady introduced herself as Mrs. Pearl and Sydney had to stifle a laugh. "Join me by the pool later, dear," Mrs. Pearl called as the elevator doors were shutting, "and I'll fill you in on all the gossip."

It's nice to see that Connors's clinic is every bit as strange as he is, Sydney thought before returning to her room to await his arrival.

CHAPTER 17

After Connors returned from his meeting with the doctor—"A nice French lad named Dr. Benoit, seemed efficient"—he and Sydney took a walk around the grounds. It was a beautiful afternoon, crystal clear and not too cold, and Connors took Sydney's arm as they strolled through the clinic's well-manicured gardens. They enjoyed the scenery while discussing their plans for later that night.

Connors said that the administrative offices for the clinic, including the dispensary, were located on the third floor of the North Wing. The records pertaining to the January project—including pharmacy logs and a list of who had booked lab time—were contained in a leather-bound book held under lock and key in the head nurse's office. "When I informed her via telephone that I would not need her assistance with the project for a while, the head nurse—as I assumed she would—asked for some time off. She won't be returning for another three days, which should give me plenty of time to take care of the problem." Connors was certain that he would be able to discern from the records which of his protégés had betrayed him.

"Why not just requisition the records yourself?" Sydney asked. "You are the director of the clinic, after all."

"We can't risk alerting the thief," he replied. "I have no idea how much of the drug they've managed to stockpile. We must obtain the records and identify the culprit without alerting them."

"All right," Sydney said, taking him at his word. "Talk to me about security. How hard is it going to be to retrieve this book?"

"Not very hard at all," he answered, "for an agent of your talents. The important thing will be to gain access to the offices and remove the book without leaving any trace of your presence."

"I'm guessing I can't just take the elevator to the third floor."

He smiled at her, looking for all the world like a proud father. "I'm afraid not. There is a guard posted outside the elevators in the lobby at night. There is one guard who periodically checks the stairwells, but they are for the most part deserted. Of course, taking the stairs wouldn't be any fun for you, would it?" he said, and gave her a wink. He waited for her to speak, encouraging her to conspire with him.

Sydney couldn't help but be charmed by this man. He seemed to instinctively know things about her that she had rarely confided to anyone like the fact that, once upon a time, she had considered her job to be fun. Before her fiancé, Danny, had been murdered on Sloane's orders, before she found out that she had been working for the bad guys, there had been a time that Sydney had enjoyed her work. She always took the job very seriously—it would be dangerous not to—but she definitely got a thrill from it. There were times in the past few years, particularly when she had been working side by side with Vaughn, that she had felt a flash of the old enjoyment, but for the most part it was more pain than pleasure. And here she was, in Switzerland, with a man she barely knew, and he was encouraging her to enjoy herself. *And why not?* she had to ask herself. *I deserve a little enjoyment.*

"Well, let's see then," she began. "Are the guards armed?"

"Not in the least. I daresay that with the exception of a few hunting rifles for the guests, you'd be hard pressed to find a weapon anywhere on the grounds."

She turned around and regarded the main building. She knew that she needed to get from the second floor of the South Wing to the third floor of the North Wing. If the elevators weren't an option, and the stairs weren't any fun, that left the outside of the building.

"What are you thinking?" he asked.

"I'm thinking I could go over the roof," she answered.

He clapped his hands in excitement. "I was hoping you'd say that. To that end, I've arranged a little assistance. When I was in the doctor's office earlier, he left me alone for a few minutes. I managed to unlock the window." He directed Sydney's attention to a window on the far end of the North

Wing, just to the side of a small balcony. "Does that look like a feasible point of entry to you?"

"I think that will do nicely," she said, getting into the spirit. "And once I'm inside the doctor's office, where do I need to go?"

"The head nurse's office is conveniently located right next to my doctor's"—he indicated another window—"and clearly marked on the door. The guard only comes through every half hour or so and apparently doesn't linger for very long."

"And what about the doors and windows—any alarms?"

"Not a one. This should be a walk in the park for you."

"I could use more walks in the park," Sydney laughed. She and Connors had come to a small pond and were making their way around the edge. Coming toward them, headed back to the clinic, was a young doctor escorting a smartly dressed elderly woman on her morning constitutional.

"The young man is Dr. Snyder," Connors whispered to Sydney. "He would be one of my newest recruits. Miss Noreen was one of our very first guests. Poor dear—there's not much left upstairs, I'm afraid."

As they passed, Dr. Snyder smiled and dipped his head toward Sydney and Connors. The woman looked a little befuddled. "Doctor?" she asked.

"No, Miss Noreen," the doctor laughed. "That's one of our new guests and his lovely daughter."

When they had moved on a bit, out of earshot of the doctor and his charge, Sydney remarked on the friendliness of the clinic's staff. "Ever since we arrived, I've been amazed with how nice they all are. It really does seem to be a wonderful place."

She wasn't exaggerating. The staff had been helpful and considerate, with no hint of the impatience and condescension that sometimes affected health-care workers. And they had been every bit as attentive to Sydney as they had been to her "father"—it was definitely impressive.

Connors sighed. "You're right, Sydney. The clinic is everything I hoped it would be when I founded it." He sounded completely miserable about it.

He guided Sydney to a stone bench overlooking the pond and sat down. She sat beside him, wondering what had caused the change in his mood.

"I have been a fool," he continued once she sat down. "I spent years trying to shield myself from other people, running from relationships of any kind. I thought that I needed that distance in order to maintain my . . . objectivity," he spit out.

Sydney didn't interrupt him. She could see that he needed to get this out. She took his hand and patted it encouragingly—as much for his benefit as to maintain their cover for the patients and staff that occasionally strolled by.

"And just look where my objectivity has gotten us," he continued bitterly. "The people in this world that I feel closest to—my students—I've never even met them face-to-face. I see them walking around these grounds, I recognize them from the video feeds, and I can't say a word to them. And now one of them has taken January—this thing that was supposed to be my penance—and turned it into a weapon."

He turned to look Sydney in the face, his eyes brimming with tears. "I spent so many years in the espionage business, Sydney—developing weapons, running these ridiculous missions—and yet it never even occurred to me that January could be put to such a use. I just assumed that everyone would look at it and see the same amazing opportunities that I see. As it turns out, all that anyone sees are dollar signs. And this is what my precious objectivity has bought me: I understand even less about human behavior than when I started."

Another coughing fit overcame Connors. It wasn't as violent as the one on the train, but it definitely left him in a weakened state. "I've been talking too much, as usual," he said when he had recovered enough. "Perhaps we should both try to get some rest before tonight's festivities."

They started back toward the main building, walking a bit slower now. They passed a few more patients—or "guests," in the preferred parlance of the clinic—on the way back. Connors identified the ones that he recognized, and was careful to point out which of the staff members they passed were potential suspects in the theft of January.

Some of the guests were accompanied by staff members, while others were on their own. Sydney noted a few, always with someone from the staff, who were younger than the average. They tended to be physically fit men and women, some of them bearing terrible scars, but all of them with the same, faraway look in their eyes. She assumed that these must be the shadow patients and Connors confirmed her suspicions.

"The poor wretches," he murmured. "Too many years in the game, and here they are: shattered minds and bodies without a soul in the world to care for them."

"Except for you and your staff," Sydney gently reminded him.

Connors smiled and thanked her. "You're very kind, Sydney . . . possibly too kind for this business. I'm glad that your father and sister and Mr. Vaughn are out there to keep an eye on you. One cannot overestimate the importance of family."

"Well, I'm not entirely incapable of looking out for myself," she laughed, "but I'm very glad that they're in my life as well." She hesitated a moment, not wanting to darken his mood further, but her curiosity got the better of her. "What about you?" she asked. "Did you ever consider having a family?"

"I *did* have a family," he answered, taking Sydney by surprise, "a wife and an infant son."

Something in the way he said the word "did" made Sydney think that it was best she not dig any deeper, but Connors continued without prompting.

"I suppose you're wondering what happened to them, and I wish that the answer were not such a shameful one," he said. "I left them—it's as simple as that. They were just two more victims of my desire for objectivity, my fear of connection. I left them and I destroyed any record of their involvement with me. I told myself that I was doing it for their sake, to protect them from the world that I was a part of." His voice trailed off and his eyes took on a look that reminded Sydney of the shadow patients. "Apparently I'm even better at lying to myself than to other people," he concluded after a long, quiet moment.

They walked on in silence for a few minutes. As they neared the greenhouse, they saw May, walking with a refined, elderly woman that Sydney assumed was her generous grandmother. They waved a friendly greeting and the sight of the women seemed to lift Connors's spirits a bit.

"Lovely," he said. "You must remind me to flirt with May's grandmother at dinner tonight. I don't see Christopher—I imagine he's gone out for a ramble on the hillside."

The greenhouse was too inviting to pass up, so they took a short detour. There was an extensive herb garden inside that had Sydney turning green with envy, and—to Connors's delight—a row of beautiful white rose bushes. "I planted these myself," he said, unable to resist the temptation of picking one of the gorgeous flowers. "I can't believe they're still here."

"Can I cut some for you?" rang out a friendly Irish-accented voice from behind Sydney and Connors. They turned to see a weathered, red-faced man in overalls, carrying a wicked-looking pair of hedge trimmers. "I'm Mr. Yates," he introduced himself, "the groundskeeper and ballroom dance instructor. Are you new to the clinic?" Once again, Sydney found herself struggling not to laugh.

They introduced themselves to Mr. Yates, and, after Sydney promised to join him on the dance floor later that evening, walked away with a bundle of beautiful roses. "Is he really the ballroom dance instructor?" Sydney whispered to Connors after they were out of earshot.

"I hope so," he replied. "I'd pay dearly to see him foxtrot in those muddy boots."

When they reached the main building, Connors proclaimed himself to be exhausted and in dire need of a nap. Sydney was eager to contact APO and was hoping for a few hours of sleep as well. They parted company at their respective rooms, agreeing to meet for an early dinner before the evening's activities.

"We can't have you breaking and entering on an empty stomach," Connors said as he was shutting the door to his room. "Sleep well, my dear."

CHAPTER 18

APO HEADQUARTERS

"I never heard of anybody named Hopkins except for that actor guy. I have no idea where the stuff came from, and it's not like I'd tell you even if I did. Who are you clowns? CIA or something like that? You guys think that you've got it all figured out, huh? You think you can just snatch a guy like me off the street and that there'll be no consequences? I got friends. I'm protected, you idiots. This place is going to be swarming with top-level brass any minute now and then we'll see who's sitting in the hot seat. You mark my words, jerks: You guys are going down and I'm going to be there to spit in your faces."

Lanchester had kept up a nonstop stream of invective since leaving Mexico, hurling insults and threats at the APO team in equal measure. There had been a brief period of respite after landing in Los Angeles, when they had placed a heavy black hood on his head—standard procedure for unauthorized personnel being brought into the APO complex—but once it was removed, he started in again with renewed vigor. He was currently sporting a sling for his dislocated shoulder and holding forth to Dixon in the interrogation cell that had just recently been vacated by Jack Bristow.

Dixon was tired and every muscle in his body ached from the fight with the giant. All he wanted to do was take a shower and see his kids. Instead he was being forced to endure a constant flood of abuse from a greasy weasel in a velour tracksuit that smelled like it hadn't been washed since disco was king. He knew that he shouldn't let Lanchester bait him, but it had been a long couple of days and his patience was entirely spent. He stood up from the table, grabbed the shackled Lanchester by the collar, and got right up in his face. "Understand me, worm. I don't, for even a minute, believe that you have friends. I doubt your own mother would cross the street to save your pathetic life. But—just supposing for a second that I might be wrong—you should know that we are completely off the books here. Your imaginary friends don't even know this place exists. Hell, you don't even exist anymore. You're screwed. So go ahead and flap your jaws, loser. It'll give me a headache, but I can take an aspirin . . . and you'll still be completely screwed."

Lanchester looked genuinely hurt and offended. "My mother loves me," he muttered.

Before Dixon had a chance to reply, Nadia opened the cell door and stuck her head in. "Dixon, Sloane wants us in his office." She almost laughed at the look of relief that washed over Dixon's face.

Upon seeing Nadia, Lanchester brightened. "Hi, beautiful," he called to her.

"Bite me," she called back as she walked away, followed closely by Dixon.

"Anything you want," Lanchester shouted as the door to his cell slammed shut.

Technically speaking, Jack Bristow was still in custody, though Sloane saw no reason to keep him locked in the holding cell. Jack had agreed to remain at APO and refrain from physically or verbally attacking his fellow agents until the completion of Sydney's mission in Switzerland. He had requested to be kept in the loop, and Sloane, who recognized the value of Jack's experience and insight, readily agreed. Jack had been keeping to himself behind his closed office door, but he joined the group in Sloane's office now for a debriefing on the Mexico City operation and a status report on what was going on at the clinic.

Jack entered Sloane's office and took a seat on one of the low couches, next to Dixon. The last time they had seen each other was when Dixon had been forced to restrain Jack from doing injury to Connors. Upon sitting, Jack clapped a hand on Dixon's shoulder and gave a slight nod of the head. Dixon smiled and nodded back. They had known each other long enough and were of sufficiently similar temperaments that this sufficed as both apology and reassurance. Sloane noticed the interaction between the two men and was pleased. He felt even more secure in his decision to release Jack from the cell.

Weiss and Nadia occupied the other couch while

Marshall hovered nervously in the doorway. Vaughn, who'd recently arrived from having his ribs taped in the medical bay and was still in a great deal of pain, sat uncomfortably on a chair in front of Sloane's desk.

"First things first," Sloane began when they were all assembled. "Excellent work in Mexico City. Preliminary reports indicate that the raid was a rousing success: millions of dollars in illegal arms confiscated, dozens of large-scale smuggling operations dismantled, and a sizeable number of *very* high-profile arrests. Congratulations are in order."

"All the credit for which will be going to someone else," remarked Vaughn, "as per usual." The pain wasn't doing much for his mood.

Sloane fixed his steely gaze on Vaughn. "Anonymity is the price that we pay for our autonomy, Agent Vaughn. Take solace in the fact that without our team the Leuba would still be in business. Will that be enough for you?"

Vaughn nodded and gritted his teeth, lamenting the fact that he couldn't take another painkiller for three more hours.

"Good," Sloane continued. "I spoke with Sydney about thirty minutes ago. She and Connors will be retrieving the records needed to identify the thief in the next few hours and will be reporting their findings back to us. We will help coordinate the apprehension of the thief and the retrieval of the drug with Swiss authorities. Where do we stand with this Lanchester character? Do we know how large a stockpile he has, or if there was anyone else involved in his operation?"

Dixon shook his head. "As far as we can determine from Interpol and CIA records, Lanchester worked solo—except, of course, for the bodyguard."

Sloane cracked the slightest of smiles as he addressed his bruised and battered agents. "It might interest you gentlemen to know that, at last count, five agents had to be hospitalized after the raid on the Leuba, all from injuries sustained while attempting to subdue Lanchester's bodyguard."

This bit of news was accepted by Dixon and Vaughn without comment, although Weiss felt compelled to speak up. "Only five?" he asked, sounding somewhat disappointed.

Ignoring Weiss, Sloane asked what information, if any, they had on Hopkins, the man who had allegedly informed Connors of the sale in the first place. "How do we know he wasn't actually involved in the sale?"

"Our intel on Hopkins is pretty nonexistent at this point," said Dixon. "Connors claims that Hopkins is an underworld contact of his, based out of London. Beyond that, we haven't been able to determine much. Lanchester denies knowing anyone of that name. But then, Lanchester also denies being a chemical weapons dealer and a scumbag. Connors was adamant that Hopkins was trustworthy and insisted that there was no way he was involved in the sale himself. Obviously it's not unthinkable that he could be playing both sides—brokering January to Lanchester and then reporting the sale to Connors—but so far we've had no luck tracking him down."

"Doesn't this strike anyone else as a bit too convenient?" Everyone in the room swiveled to face Jack as he spoke up for the first time in the meeting. Vaughn rubbed his broken ribs and considered questioning Jack's definition of the word "convenient," but thought better of it as Jack continued speaking. "It's all so neat, so tidy. When have you ever known this sort of thing to be neat and tidy?"

Sloane took a deep breath, hoping that Jack

wasn't going to relapse into the raging madman of the day before. "I understand your concern, Jack, but the fact remains that Connors's intel was good. The market was where he said it would be and January *was* on offer there. I think we have to proceed on the assumption that he has been straight with us up to this point."

Jack opened his mouth to protest, but Sloane cut him off by dismissing the briefing. "You had a long night, people. Relax, shut your eyes for a couple of hours, but no one goes home until Sydney has completed her mission and we've recovered this drug. Marshall . . . I'll see you in your office in a few minutes."

Once the others had vacated his office, Sloane turned to Jack, his eyes full of sympathy. "I really do understand, Jack. I know that this isn't easy for you."

"Arvin—," Jack began, but Sloane held up his hand to indicate that he hadn't finished.

"I think of how it must be for Sydney and Marcus—and for you—having to work alongside me, in spite of the . . . things . . . that I've done." The words were difficult for him to say, but Sloane felt it was important for Jack to hear them. "I know that there are situations where forgiveness is out of the question. I understand that. But that doesn't preclude the possibility of change, does it? The possibility of a true and genuine change of heart?"

When Jack spoke, his voice was perfectly controlled, without a hint of the fury that had blinded him before. "And *you* are willing to gamble Sydney's life on this . . . possibility?"

Sloane knew Jack well enough to understand the unspoken implication in what he said: If Sloane *was* willing to gamble on this possibility, Jack would hold him personally responsible for whatever happened to Sydney. The man behind the desk considered his words carefully before replying.

"You know that if I thought anything were amiss, I would abort the mission and get Sydney out of there immediately. But until that situation arises, I see no option besides completing our assignment. To that end, I think that we should find out what Marshall has managed to uncover." That was Arvin Sloane, the director of APO, speaking. His expression softened a little, and Arvin Sloane, sometime friend to Jack Bristow, had the final word. "I need to believe that people can change, Jack. And I need to know that you believe it too."

Jack didn't reply, and his face gave nothing away.

CHAPTER 19

LONDON

Mrs. Davis, Angela to her friends and boarders, shuffled to the stairs in her slippers and housecoat and cocked her head to listen for a moment. She assured herself that she wasn't being nosy; she was merely . . . curious. Mrs. Davis prided herself on the fact that she had never, in more than forty years of renting rooms in her four-story semidetached house in Kensington, pried into the business of her lodgers—not even the two girls in number six who had gone out at night dressed in a certain way and had no visible means of support, and not the man in number twelve whose gentleman callers came and went at all hours, and certainly not the man in number three who kept a large stash of a certain type of magazine beneath his mattress. No—Mrs. Davis was definitely *not* the type to trouble herself with the affairs of others. *Live and let live, I always say. It's certainly no concern of mine. . . . I wonder what they're doing up there?*

Twenty minutes earlier, two men had rung the bell and asked to see the quiet man in number thirteen. They were well-dressed men in suits and ties and raincoats—not like that troublemaker in number seven with the torn jeans and the leather jacket—and she let them into the foyer. They had assured Mrs. Davis, who insisted that they call her Angela, that her lodger was expecting them and that there was no need to buzz for him. They seemed like nice men and, since Angela's favorite television program was just beginning, she saw no harm in pointing the way to the stairs and sending them up. But now, twenty minutes later, her curiosity—which was definitely not the same thing as nosiness—had gotten the better of her. The quiet man in number thirteen had *never* received visitors before—not that she was keeping track, mind you—and Angela was . . . curious. *I wonder what they're talking about.*

The television program had been forgotten entirely. She started up the stairs, ignoring that nagging little voice in her head that was constantly reminding her of what it was that had killed the cat.

Hopkins had been taken completely unawares. He had just come from the bathroom down the hall and was gathering his wallet and keys in preparation for going out for the night. He heard the familiar squeak of the second stair from the top but assumed that, as per usual, the monumentally nosy Mrs. Davis was just keeping tabs on his whereabouts. He hadn't pulled the door shut behind himself because he was not planning on staying, and so he was unprepared for the sight of two men with silenced pistols aimed at his head when he turned around.

Hopkins was very familiar with guns—they were his bread and butter, as it were—but having one, not to mention two, pointed at him was a completely new experience. *They look much bigger from this angle,* he thought. "Nine-millimeter Berettas . . . very reliable," was what he said out loud.

The two men stepped into the room and closed the door. The larger of the two remained at the door while his companion crossed the room and took a seat at the small dining table. He gestured with his pistol for Hopkins to sit in the other chair and Hopkins saw no sense in declining the invitation.

It occurred to Hopkins as he was sitting that he had no idea why these men were here. He wasn't so foolish as to believe that they were in his room by mistake—he just wasn't sure *which* of his many schemes had gone wrong. He didn't have to wonder for long.

"Please don't speak for the moment. I'm going to explain to you, very carefully, what it is that we already know. And then you are going to fill in the gaps in our knowledge. And whether or not you live, and how much of your body remains intact, depends entirely on how quickly you fill in those gaps. Do you understand?" The man's voice was quiet and calm, and as he spoke, he removed several items from the pockets of his raincoat and set them on the table: a red rubber ball, a roll of packing tape, a fountain pen, a small notebook, and a large folding knife.

Hopkins nodded to indicate that he understood

and the man smiled. “Good. Do you know how to write?” Another nod and the man stood up and walked around behind Hopkins’s chair and pressed the barrel of his gun to the base of Hopkins’s skull. “Excellent. I want you to place the ball in your mouth, Mr. Hopkins.” Again, the sensible course of action seemed to be compliance.

Once the ball was in place—no small feat in itself—the man with the gun grabbed the roll of tape off the table and secured the gag with two or three quick spins around Hopkins’s head. He didn’t bother to tear off the tape when he had finished and just left the roll dangling down Hopkins’s back. Hopkins’s mouth was entirely sealed off. It occurred to him that if he had still been suffering from the cold that had plagued him the week previously, he would be completely unable to breathe at this point.

The man returned to the seat opposite Hopkins and motioned for his associate to join them at the table. The second man took up position behind Hopkins, making a great show of bending over the gagged man’s shoulder to retrieve the knife from the table and then snapping it open next to his ear.

“Here’s what we know,” the first man began,

making good on his earlier promise. "You provided a drug, some kind of chemical something-or-other, to a loudmouthed weasel named Lanchester. The weasel in question then used this drug to gain a spot at a very exclusive, very prestigious gathering of people with such things to sell. This gathering was subsequently disrupted by the authorities and the weasel was seen being escorted from the premises by a group of people that turned out to be agents of the United States. Are you following me?"

Hopkins nodded and reached up to wipe away the sweat that was beading up on his forehead. *At least now I know which deal we're talking about.*

"Very good, now pay attention. My employer—who is not only the man who ran the aforementioned gathering, but also my cousin—is currently languishing in a filthy Mexican prison and he is very upset about that fact. He has instructed me to determine who is responsible for this situation."

Hopkins attempted to protest his innocence at this point, but only managed a muffled grunt. The man at the table held up his hand for silence.

"We know that it isn't your fault. All that you did, to your misfortune, was broker a chemical weapon to a man who seems to be constitutionally incapable of keeping his mouth shut. As it turns out, Mr. Lanchester told just about anyone who would listen that he had acquired a fantastic new weapon from a man in London named Hopkins. A quick check with some associates of mine revealed that you would have only been a middle man in such a deal. My employer has learned, through channels you needn't worry about, that it was the original source of said chemical that was responsible for wrecking his party. So what I'm going to need from you is a name and a location. I cannot stress to you how important it is—important for *you*—that you provide me with that information quickly and truthfully."

With that, the first man nodded to his companion, who again leaned over Hopkins's shoulder in order to adjust the articles on the table. He opened the notebook and placed the pen in Hopkins's right hand. He then twisted Hopkins's left arm behind his back and began to sever the little finger from Hopkins's left hand with the knife.

Hopkins was not a particularly brave man, and he had a serious aversion to pain. But he also considered the man that these goons were looking for to be his friend—and so he did his best to shield his friend from them. He blinked away the tears of pain that had filled his eyes and struggled to remain conscious while he wrote two words on the blank notebook page in front of him.

The man at the table reached across and spun the notebook around so that he could read what Hopkins had written. "Jackson. Madrid. You're saying that we should be looking for a man named Jackson in Madrid? Madrid, Spain?" Hopkins nodded weakly. The man ripped out the page, balled it up, and threw it on the floor. He spun the notebook back around and pushed it in front of Hopkins. "I don't think so. Let's see what we come up with this time." This time, the big man removed two fingers as Hopkins wrote a different name and location. It wasn't long before the big man had to move beyond fingers.

It took four sheets of paper before the man at the table believed that Hopkins was being truthful. Each time, he demanded that Hopkins be a little more detailed in his description. Before the third sheet, he and his partner had to splash water in Hopkins's face to revive him. Hopkins knew in his heart that the men were never going to let him live, and he felt ashamed of his weakness as he wrote down exactly what they wanted to know.

Just before Hopkins lost consciousness for the final time, he heard a squeak from the floorboards on the landing outside his door. The last thing he ever saw, just as everything was fading to black, was the big man crossing to the door, blood-stained knife in hand. *Poor Mrs. Davis,* he thought, and breathed his last breath.

CHAPTER 20

APO HEADQUARTERS

Marshall Flinkman was genuinely baffled and, for the first time in his life, was completely happy about it. January was displaying all of the subtleties and complexities that one would expect from a drug designed by the Ghost. It was definitely not about to yield its secrets without a fight—and Marshall would have been disappointed if it had.

"I can't even tell you what an honor it is for me to be doing this. Seriously . . . I've never approached an analysis with such a sense of awe and . . . and . . . privilege before. It's a pretty amazing feeling. Like . . . you know how you think about how the first man on the moon is going to feel? The real first man, I mean, not the fake ones that they . . . not that it would have to be a man, mind you. I really don't see why they couldn't send a woman once they finally decide to—"

"The analysis, Marshall. What can you tell us?" Sloane had even less patience for his underling's ramblings than usual. He and Jack were crowded into Marshall's cluttered workshop awaiting the results of a battery of tests that had begun the minute the team had returned from Mexico City with the sample.

Currently a test tube containing a small amount of the substance was being spun at enormous speed in a tabletop centrifuge in an attempt to separate its constituent elements according to molecular weight while another sample was brought to a boil over the flame of a gas burner. The results of these tests, along with a handful of others, were being fed electronically into the imposing bank of computers that dominated the room. A small wooden rack holding three more tubes sat on Marshall's desk, awaiting the next round of analysis.

Marshall stared blankly at Sloane for a moment, completely mystified by the idea that not everyone was as enthralled by this moment as he was. He was only brought back to reality by the startling sound of an African bull elephant trumpeting—the signal that his computer had completed the initial analysis.

"Let's see what we've got here," Marshall said excitedly as spun in his chair to face the monitors. "Well, right off the bat, I can tell you that this sample has been highly diluted. You see these bars here? That's water, basically."

"What about the rest?" Jack seemed every bit as impatient as Sloane.

"It's not really like anything that I've seen before . . . which is hardly surprising, considering the source." He spun back around to face Jack and Sloane. "Did you know that the Ghost once managed to synthesize the aroma of a freshly baked apple pie in order to mask a deadly dose of—" The look on Jack's face stopped Marshall in mid-sentence. He turned back to the monitors. "Like I said, it's not like anything I've seen before. Or, more accurately, it's like *everything* I've seen before."

"What do you mean?" Sloane asked, wishing that for just once in his life, Marshall would cut to the chase.

"There is a whole list of things in there: trace amounts of metals and pollens and a bunch of stuff I haven't even identified yet, little bit of lead, little bit of what seems to be rust but is probably something else entirely—nothing that seems out of the ordinary by itself, but there's no telling how these things will react when you combine them. It's like that fruit salad with the pineapple and the cherries and the little marshmallows but hopefully without the shredded coconut. It sounds terrible, but—"

"Forget the fruit salad, Marshall. Is this substance what . . . that man . . . said it was?" Jack was still unable to bring himself to utter Connors's name.

"Well . . . I don't know . . . yet. It's a complicated substance. It's not the kind of thing that is just going to . . ." Marshall's voice was rising in pitch with each question that he was unable to answer.

Jack cut him off. "Is this some kind of powerful hallucinogen or not?"

Marshall's forehead had broken out into a cold

sweat and he looked as if he were about to drop dead of a heart attack. “I don’t know,” he squealed. “But, Mr. Bristow, why would Connors have lied about that?”

The reply was quick and to the point. “Because that is what he does. He lies,” Jack said, and then brought his fist down on the wooden rack holding the remaining samples of January.

The rack and the three test tubes shattered beneath Jack’s hand. A sliver of glass pierced his skin and a tiny rivulet of blood mixed with the puddle of clear liquid that was spreading quickly across Marshall’s desk. Before either Sloane or Marshall could react, Jack dipped a finger in the liquid and put it to his lips. “Tap water,” he declared with a bitter note of triumph in his voice.

“Marshall.” Sloane spoke through clenched teeth. “Put us into lockdown: level-four biohazard.”

Marshall was in shock. “I built that rack in eighth-grade wood shop,” he moaned.

“Marshall!” Sloane barked, snapping Marshall out of his despair.

“Got it: level-four biohazard . . . coming right up.” Marshall turned to his keyboard to access the complex’s emergency shutdown controls.

"Marshall, if you lock us down, Sydney will die." Jack's words stopped Marshall cold. "Arvin," he continued, turning to Sloane, "it was bait. That's all it was. January doesn't exist. It never existed. You have to let me go to Switzerland."

Sloane shook his head. "I can't risk it, Jack. We've got to seal this place off. There are too many lives at stake here."

"No one's life is at stake except for Sydney's. There was nothing in those tubes except for water. Marshall, you said so yourself."

"I said that it was mostly water," Marshall replied meekly. His hands were still poised over his keyboard, waiting for some sort of definitive instructions.

"Arvin, if you lock us down, we are quarantined for seventy-two hours. Sydney doesn't have that long. Please, I'm begging you. As a father, as a friend—don't do this."

Sloane held Jack's gaze for a moment and then turned to Marshall. "Look at that analysis again. Is it possible that this substance is water?" Marshall had already turned back to the screen and was scrolling through the data.

"Water? No way. I don't think . . . what I mean

to say is . . ." Marshall looked up from the computer. "Well, now that I look at it again, I suppose that it could be some kind of"—his face wrinkled in revulsion—"unfiltered tap water. Nothing you would want to drink though."

Sloane absorbed this news, considering his options. "Marshall, will you step out into the hall for a moment?" he asked. It didn't even occur to Marshall until he was outside and the door had been shut that he had just been kicked out of his own office.

When they were alone, Sloane turned to Jack. "I'm sorry that I doubted you. I should have known better."

"I understand. I haven't been at my best," said Jack with masterful understatement.

"Who do you want to take with you?" Sloane asked, getting down to business.

"No one," Jack answered. "Let me handle this myself."

Sloane nodded, knowing full well what Jack meant by "handle." "I'll arrange a flight," he said.

"Make it a fast one," was Jack's terse response.

CHAPTER 21

SWITZERLAND

True to his word, Connors spent a good chunk of the dinner hour flirting with May's grandmother—as well as with several other female diners. Leaving Sydney alone at their table, he made his way around the spacious, wood-paneled dining hall, meeting people and generally having a fine old time.

Sydney had a cup of coffee with her dessert—the best piece of apple pie that she had ever eaten—and reflected on the past few days. In spite of the seriousness of their mission and the troubling situation with her father, she was actually enjoying herself, and her job, for the first time in a long while. Connors was entertaining and had a knack for making even the most mundane of events into something exciting. And it was certainly a relief to be infiltrating a facility that wasn't surrounded by armed guards or wired to explode at any second.

But there was also a melancholy side to her thoughts. The hours on the train she'd spent "reminiscing" with Connors and their companions had left her with a dull ache inside. It pained her to think that most of her family memories involved guns and killing and betrayal instead of trips to the Grand Canyon and talking wooden Indians. She vowed that when she returned to Los Angeles, she was going to make more of an effort to appreciate the family that she had. She was going to spend more time with Nadia. And no matter how difficult it was going to be, she was determined to have a closer, more trusting relationship with her father.

It was troubling to think that it took the appearance of a mysterious man that she had never met for her to learn about what was plainly one of the defining events in her father's life. As she had said to Sloane, there was no question in Sydney's mind that her father loved her and that he would do anything to protect her. When he had learned that Irina Derevko—Sydney's mother and the love of Jack's life—had been arranging to have Sydney killed, Jack had not hesitated before putting a bullet in her head. But in spite of his obvious love for his daughter, he was very good at keeping her at arm's length and constantly avoided revealing too much about himself. As strange as it seemed, Sydney had never even seen where her father lived. *That kind of thing is not going to happen anymore,* she thought. *We are a family. And maybe one of these days Vaughn and I will add to that family.*

The thought of Vaughn brought a smile to her lips, even though she was worried about him. She had talked to Sloane before dinner and had learned that Vaughn had been injured in the raid on the arms market. In spite of Sloane's reassurances that it was only a few cracked ribs—a painful but ultimately minor injury of a sort that both she and Vaughn had faced before—she couldn't help but wish that she were home to take care of him.

Her thoughts were interrupted by Connors's return to the table. "Still feeling tired, darling?" he inquired, loud enough for several neighboring tables to hear. "Let's get you back up to the room so that you can lie down."

Ever since learning that the Mexico City operation had been a rousing success, Connors had been in a buoyantly good mood. He escorted Sydney to the South Wing elevators with a spring in his step, whistling the whole way.

Once they were upstairs, Sydney excused herself in order to change clothes. She donned her skintight black tactical gear and spent a few minutes stretching and limbering up. Tonight's operation was not particularly risky compared to some missions she'd executed, but it promised to be a bit of a workout.

When she was ready, she strapped on the black webbed belt that carried the tools she was going to need, grabbed the detachable hood of her tactical suit, and rejoined Connors in his room. He wished her luck—not that she was going to need it, of course—and invited her to join him in the main lounge area once she had completed her task. "Unless of course you're still feeling too tired, darling," he said with a wink.

She laughed and promised to join him for a nightcap in just a little while. Connors doffed an imaginary hat to her and exited the room. Sydney took a few deep breaths, then opened the sliding door to the balcony.

It was cold outside, but Sydney was completely comfortable in the insulated suit. She pulled the hood down over her head so that the only part of her body exposed to the elements was a narrow band across her eyes. It was a dark, cloudy night and she took a few moments to let her eyes adjust. She stood at the railing of the balcony, perfectly still, and looked out over the grounds of the clinic. When she was sure that there was no one wandering below who might look up and see her, she stepped onto the railing, took a second to find her balance, and then jumped up to catch the lip of the balcony above.

She hung from the third-floor balcony for a few seconds, enjoying the stretch, and then flexed her arms and pulled herself up so that she could get a better grip on the railing. Once she had a firm grasp, she swung her right leg up and hooked her heel over the top railing. She used her arms and her leg to lever herself up and rolled silently over the top railing, landing in a crouch on the balcony.

The balcony was identical to the one below,

with two sliding glass doors opening into adjoining rooms. Both rooms were dark and had the curtains drawn over the doors. Hopefully the occupants were soundly asleep or, like Connors, enjoying the amenities of the lounge. She made her way to the far end of the balcony and again stepped up onto the top railing.

She was a few feet away from a metal rain pipe that ran from the roof gutters to the ground below. She had taken a good look at the pipe that afternoon; it had appeared to be sturdy, and, most importantly, firmly anchored to the building. She bent forward at the waist and extended her arms until she got a grip on the pipe. It felt solid, but she wouldn't know for sure until it was too late to do anything about it. She tightened her grip and transferred all of her weight from her legs to her arms. She took a breath, and then gracefully swung her legs across the gap and braced her feet against the wall, taking some of the strain off her arms. The pipe didn't even budge.

Sydney let out a sigh of relief, and then started up the pipe to the roof. Her boots didn't afford much purchase against the smooth metal, so her hands and arms had to do most of the work. She found herself marveling at the new gloves with the rubberized palms that Marshall had developed on his lunch break a few weeks previous. *I have to remember to thank him when I get back,* she thought. *These things are amazing.*

It only took her a few seconds to shinny up to the point where she could reach the gutter, but upon inspection it didn't seem as sturdy as the pipe. She climbed a little higher, enough to get the upper half of her torso above the gutter, and then reached out with her right hand for a vent cover that was set two feet back from the edge of the roof. Her fingers just barely reached the lip of the vent, but it was enough. She curled the tips of her fingers around the edge, then let go of the pipe with her left hand and grabbed the vent. Straining her arms and shoulders, she managed to get the top half of her body above the gutter and onto the roof. She caught her breath, and then pulled herself all the way up.

Sydney rested for a second against one of the decorative gables that topped the North and South Wings, and then made her way to the peak of the gently sloping roof. From here it was an easy walk along the peak to the steep, A-frame roof of the center section. She reached the center with no trouble, and then took a second to prepare herself for the next leg of her trip.

The roof towered above her, the steep sides rising to a point in the center. She started walking up one of the steeply angled wooden beams that made up the framework, her arms outstretched like a wire walker's, for balance. On either side of the beam were the enormous panes of thick glass that served as a skylight for the main hall below. Sydney could plainly see people lounging around in front of the fireplace and engaging in various leisure activities, but she wasn't worried—she was far enough away that the black clothing and the moonless night rendered her all but invisible. She was relieved to note that her boots, which hadn't been of much use climbing the pipe, gripped the weathered wood nicely.

The beam was almost a foot wide, and there wasn't any wind, so Sydney's main concern was the strain on her legs. She had been expecting it, but the reality was tougher than she imagined. When she was halfway up the first side, her calves and thighs were burning like a marathon runner's. To keep her mind off the pain, she looked through the windows beneath her, trying to spot Connors. It wasn't very difficult; even from five stories above, his blue and white seersucker suit was distinctive. Sydney even fancied that she could make out a tiny spot of white on his lapel where the ever-present rose would be.

Connors was engaged in a chess game with someone—Sydney guessed from the top of his head that it was Christopher. The sight of Connors playing chess—the very game that had figured so prominently in her father's recounting of the events in Viet Nam—sent a chill up her spine, and her father's voice echoed in her ears. She couldn't help but wonder if she was being foolish, trusting Connors in spite of everything that her father had said.

The final push to the top was excruciating. The thought that, when she formulated this plan, she and Connors had been discussing ways to make tonight more "fun" was almost enough to make her laugh.

She made it to the peak of the roof and had to rest for a few minutes until the burning in her legs subsided a bit. She could just make out the lights of Lucerne, twinkling far in the distance. Sydney was grateful for the lack of moonlight—it certainly lessened her chances of being spotted—but she was fairly sure that, had she been able to see out over the mountains and the lake from her vantage point, the view might have been spectacular enough to justify any amount of leg pain necessary to get there.

The descent from the central peak to the roof of the North Wing posed a whole new set of difficulties. An entirely different group of muscles was called into play and Sydney was forced to lean backward in order to prevent herself from succumbing to the force of gravity and rolling down the roof. Every step was a challenge, and Sydney was tempted to sit down and scoot her way to the bottom. She soon realized that it was much easier to turn around and back down the beam, but the strain was still intense. By the time she reached the bottom, her legs felt like noodles. She allowed herself to sit for a few minutes before continuing, trying not to think about the return trip.

Looking through the windows, she noted that the chess game appeared to be over. Christopher was nowhere in sight and Connors had joined a table of undoubtedly charmed women near the fireplace.

Ignoring the dull protests of her thighs and calves, Sydney stood and made her way across the roof of the North Wing to the far end of the building. She lay down on the roof and worked her legs over the side, inching down until she could grip the edge of the roof with her hands. She lowered herself to the full extent of her arms, grateful to relieve her legs of all weight for a moment, and then dropped to the balcony below, landing with barely a sound.

Connors's plan worked perfectly. The window was still unlocked and the doctor's office was deserted. There was a frosted glass pane in the door of the office and through it Sydney could tell that the hallway beyond was dark. She crossed to the door, quietly unlocked it, and eased it open—the hallway was deserted. The only illumination was provided by a pair of red exit signs, one at either end of the long corridor.

She ducked out and made her way to the office door marked HEAD NURSE in bold letters on the frosted glass pane. She tried the door—locked, of course. She pulled a small flashlight and her lock picks from the tool pouch on her belt and got to work. The door was open in a matter of seconds and she slipped into the office, locking the door behind her.

She went to work on the filing cabinet and in no time at all felt the tumblers fall into place and heard the satisfying *click* of the lock disengaging. *I could have done this with a hairpin,* she thought as she rifled through the drawers.

The book that Connors had described was in the back of the bottom drawer, underneath a metal cashbox. It was a beautiful brown leather-bound volume with Connors's patron, the familiar two-headed god, embossed on the cover. It was filled with page after page of tiny, flowery script. There were hand-drawn charts and diagrams and literally hundreds of variations on a chemical formula that Sydney assumed must be January. The pharmacy log was on the back two pages, but Sydney couldn't make heads or tails of the head nurse's arcane notation system.

She unzipped a small pouch on her belt and removed a compacted black rucksack. She slipped the book inside and slung it over her shoulder, then carefully closed the cabinet and locked it.

Sydney had originally planned to return to her room by the same route that she came. But now, with her legs aching and her arms and shoulders not much better, she was rethinking that plan. *Isn't tonight supposed to be about having fun? It was a nice workout the first time, but tackling that roof again? No, thank you.*

Connors had said that the guards were posted at the elevator doors on the ground floor. Presumably Sydney could make it down the emergency stairwell that far, and then she would have to find some way to slip across the main floor and make it to the stairs for the South Wing. If necessary, she supposed she could exit through a ground-floor window somewhere and try to reach her second-floor balcony from outside. Not the best option, maybe, but she had certainly faced worse in her day. The elevator was an attractive choice, considering the state of her leg muscles, but the chance of alerting the guard in the lobby was too great. "The stairs it is," she muttered under her breath, not relishing the thought.

She stepped through the door and gently pulled it shut behind her. The *click* of the lock engaging sounded as loud as a gunshot in the quiet hallway, but Sydney was the only one around to hear it.

She moved quickly past the elevators to the far

end of the hall, toward the exit sign that marked the stairs down to the lobby. Just as she reached the stairwell door, the elevator chimed behind her and the doors slid open, spilling light into the hallway.

Sydney grabbed for the door handle and eased it open, as silently and quickly as possible. She slipped inside the stairwell and softly closed the door behind her—holding the crash bar down so that the latch wouldn't catch—just as the voice of the elevator's occupant cut through the silence.

"Is that better? I'm out of the elevator. . . . Yeah, I can hear you."

Whoever was speaking—it was a man's voice—was moving down the hallway toward the stairwell. Through the small, rectangular window above the door handle Sydney saw the fluorescent lights in the hallway ceiling flicker to life. She held her breath and crouched down, still keeping the latch from clicking shut.

"How long ago?" the unseen man asked, apparently talking to someone on a cell phone. His voice was accompanied by the jangling sound of a ring of keys being removed from a pocket. "You're sure?" he inquired after a moment, coming to a stop right outside the stairwell.

The jangle of keys was followed by the sound of a door being unlocked. Sydney breathed a sigh of relief; the unseen man was entering the office across the hall. He didn't close the door behind him and she could still make out what he was saying.

"Do we have any idea how many men they're sending?" the man asked, a definite note of fear in his voice. It sounded like he was frantically digging through drawers and cabinets as he spoke. Only now did it strike Sydney how familiar the voice sounded.

"May is here," the voice said. "She's with a patient right now." It was Christopher speaking.

Sydney's mind reeled and she felt like she'd been punched in the stomach. She quickly ran through a handful of scenarios in her mind—all of which led her to the same troubling conclusion. If Christopher and May were on the clinic's staff, there was no way that Connors wouldn't have known who they were. The warning voice in her head—which had begun to sound exactly like her father over the past few days—was echoing so loudly that it almost drowned out Christopher.

"I'll let him know. Thank you," Christopher was

saying. "I just hope that we can repay the favor someday."

She listened as Christopher hung up his phone and stepped back into the hallway. She steeled herself, ready to subdue him if he chose to exit via the stairwell, but he locked the office door and moved back toward the elevators. The door chimed, the hallway lights flickered off, and the third floor was quiet again.

Sydney relaxed her death grip on the crash bar and let the door latch pop shut. She leaned against the wall and tried to take stock of her situation, but her thoughts were tumbling over one another faster than she could process them. Clearly this mission was not what it seemed—this place was not what it seemed, these people were not who they seemed—and it didn't take a rocket scientist to figure out the identity of the man behind the curtain. That pesky voice in her head—her father's voice—took on a tone of *I told you so* satisfaction.

Her initial instinct was to get out. She could hotwire one of the clinic's vehicles, make her way back to Taviston, and hole up somewhere after calling for reinforcements. Connors and his cronies might appear relatively harmless on the surface, but the thought of her father and the ill-fated Nha Trang team argued strongly against that assumption.

And yet, there was a part of Sydney that still wanted to trust Connors. What if her instincts were wrong? What if Connors had no idea who Christopher and May were and Sydney was leaving him in jeopardy if she fled? Her father's voice scolded her and began rattling off a laundry list of people that she had mistakenly trusted in the past. *Sloane, your mother* . . . She shook her head to shut him up. "You're not helping right now," she whispered, briefly wondering if talking out loud to the voices in her head was enough to earn her a permanent spot at the Devereaux.

Obviously, the right thing to do was get out, call for help, and wait for the APO team to arrive. Just the thought of leaving the clinic made her father's voice downgrade from "warning" to "approval" level in her mind. There was absolutely no doubt about it: Getting out now was the safest course of action. Sydney stood up, took a deep breath, and—not for the first time in her life—decided to ignore the safest course of action.

CHAPTER 22

The question of whether Connors knew who Christopher and May were was answered the moment that Sydney entered Connors's room through the balcony door.

The return trip was far less physically taxing than the maiden voyage over the roof had been. Sydney had made her way down the stairwell to the first floor without incident. She had avoided the lobby—sparsely populated at this hour, but still a risk—by cutting back through the North Wing and exiting the building at the far end, three stories below the window that she had used to enter the offices.

She had circled around the back of the building, doing her best to remain in the shadows, and reached the South Wing without encountering another soul. She'd then used the lower portion of the same drain pipe that had aided in her initial ascent to get within reach of the balcony railing. Finally she had pulled herself up and over the edge and onto the balcony.

Connors's window was ablaze with light. The drapes had not been drawn and Sydney could hear voices from inside—it sounded like two men—but she couldn't tell what they were saying through the glass and wood. She removed her hood but still couldn't make out the words. She moved quietly to the door, her presence on the balcony hidden by the bundle of the drapes, and risked a peek around the edge. Reflected in the mirror over the dresser she could see Christopher, standing in the open hallway door. Connors was sitting on the bed, looking pale and haggard—and repeatedly shaking his head in disbelief.

Sydney decided to grab the bull by the horns. She once again bid her father's nagging voice to be silent, grabbed the door handle, and slid the door open.

Connors barely reacted at all. He seemed to Sydney to have resigned himself to some awful fate that only he understood, but Christopher sputtered and coughed and basically did the worst job of covering up that Sydney had ever witnessed.

"Oh, hey . . . Ms. Connors. We were just . . . your father and I were . . . um . . . I should go," he stammered, and started to back out of the room, attempting to pull the door shut as he went.

"Christopher . . . it's okay," Connors said quietly. "Look at Sydney's face. We aren't fooling anyone. Come back in and shut the door."

Christopher looked sheepish, but he did as he was told.

Sydney remained in the open doorway, not sure whether she would need to make a quick exit. Connors looked up at her and smiled sadly.

"I can understand your hesitation, Sydney, but I assure you that there's no need to stand there freezing. Please come in. There is a lot that needs to be said . . . and not very much time to say it."

"Will any of it be the truth?" Sydney asked.

Connors locked eyes with her, and for just a

moment Sydney saw a hint of the sparkle that seemed to have vanished from his eyes. When he finally spoke, it was in the weariest voice that Sydney had ever heard.

"I suppose, as a last resort, that the truth has become a necessity. Although it isn't really my area of expertise, I'm afraid."

Sydney stepped into the room and slid the door shut behind her. "Give it a try," she said.

It took nearly an hour for Connors to come clean—and when he had finished, Sydney was afraid that she might be no closer to knowing the truth than when he began. A call to APO brought an assurance from Sloane that reinforcements were on the way, but that did little to allay Sydney's fears. If Connors *was* telling the truth, the good guys would never arrive in time. If Connors was still lying . . . she had no idea what to think. The thought that she might be the unwitting subject of some elaborate experiment still hovered in the back of her mind, and she struggled to push it away. *Better to not even go down that path.*

Connors had begun his confession by insisting that a lot of what he had already told her was the truth. His name *was* Reginald Connors, he *had* abandoned his wife and son, and there was indeed a drug called January that would do everything that he said it would. The clinic operated in much the same fashion as he had described, with one crucial difference. "I am in fact the director of this clinic. I have lived here and supervised the entire operation from day one."

Sydney was now sitting at a small table near the window, across from Connors, who remained on the edge of the bed. "So how come no one recognizes you? Do you run the whole thing from some secret command center in the basement?"

He laughed a little at this, but did his best to keep the proceedings serious. "You probably aren't going to like this part," he began. Sydney considered informing him that she didn't like *any* part of what was happening, but thought better of it and allowed him to continue. "When I left here a few days ago, I informed the staff—and a few select patients—that I would be returning from America with a deeply delusional young woman."

Sydney could see just where he was headed. "You have got to be kidding me," she sighed.

"I'm afraid not," he went on. "I was to return with a young woman who believed that any man of a certain age was her father—her father who had died of cancer two years previous. I was going to persuade this young woman—you, Sydney—that 'her father's' best hope for recovery was an experimental program at an exclusive clinic in Switzerland."

"I thought that everyone did an excellent job," Christopher spoke up, and immediately looked as if he regretted calling attention to himself.

"You're very right, Christopher. I must remember to thank them all," Connors said, then added a quiet postscript, "if the sun rises tomorrow."

"And just who are you, exactly? One of the protégés, I assume," Sydney addressed Christopher.

"Not exactly," Christopher replied, but declined to elaborate.

"There are no protégés, Sydney, and Christopher, I say with great pride, is my son." Connors was practically beaming.

Sydney raised an eyebrow, but didn't say anything, so Connors attempted to fill in a few more blanks.

"Yes . . . the very same son that I abandoned more than thirty years ago. A powerful combination of guilt and curiosity got the better of me a few years ago and I sought out the family that I had discarded." His eyes filled with tears that quickly spilled over. Christopher sat down on the bed—his own eyes tearing up—and took his father's hand as the old man struggled with the words. "My . . . wife . . . had passed on, but I had the good fortune to meet this young man." Connors planted a kiss on top of Christopher's head, and Sydney found herself believing that they were indeed father and son.

Connors composed himself and went on. "I was amazed to learn that Christopher had followed my footsteps into medicine—albeit in a far more admirable way—and even more amazed to find that he wanted to make my acquaintance after all those years." Connors paused, his lips trembling from the strain of holding back from sobbing. "He immediately accepted me, with all the love that I could ever ask for. When I think that it took me thirty years to find that kind of . . ." The strain proved too strong for Connors and he let go, his words dissolving in a flood of tears.

He sobbed in his son's arms for a good minute before regaining enough control to speak at all—and then only enough to apologize to Sydney for his outburst. She gave him time to calm down, and then encouraged him to go on with his story.

Dabbing at his eyes with his ever-present handkerchief, Connors continued. "I was able to persuade Christopher to join me in my work here at the clinic . . . where he met May."

"Let me guess," Sydney interjected. "That was May's office I broke into tonight?"

Connors nodded and confirmed her suspicion. "She has been with me as a nurse for many years now. You can't imagine how happy I was to see love blossom between the two people that I hold dearest to my heart."

"How cozy for all of you," Sydney said with more than a little bitterness. "So, what happened? One day you all just got bored and decided to mess with my father and me? Is this your idea of family bonding?"

"That's not fair," Christopher said quietly.

Sydney snorted derisively. "Not fair? Do you really want to start a discussion about fairness with me under these circumstances?"

Connors interrupted. "Sydney . . . I'm dying."

It was the simplest statement that Sydney had ever heard from him, and the first that she didn't even question. More than the coughing and the weakness, there was a look in his eyes that no one—not Sloane, not her mother—would have been able to fake. It was the look of a man who had fallen in love with life, perhaps for the first time ever, and was then told that it was over. Connors was dying—of that, she was sure. And that knowledge softened her feelings toward him.

"I'm sorry," she said, truthfully. "But I still don't understand . . ."

"Some months ago," Connors continued, "right around the time that I was diagnosed as terminal, I was approached by two men—representatives of some intelligence agency or another—and questioned about the possibility of using January as a weapon. You must believe me—I had never even considered the possibility. What I told you before was the truth. I do not engage in that sort of activity anymore. I'm not even sure how they got wind of my experiments in the first place."

"So then, why the charade? Why get *me* here to steal something from your own offices?"

"Because later this evening, had things gone according to plan, you were to witness my death. And my work and I were going to disappear forever." Connors gave a bitter laugh at this point. "As it turns out, that may still be the case."

"How so?" Sydney inquired.

Christopher chimed in with the answer. "Because a team of men have been dispatched from Zurich to kill him. I'm sorry, Miss Bristow. I know that what we did was wrong, but right now we need to forego the apologies and explanations and concentrate on getting my father to safety."

Connors laid a reassuring hand on Christopher's arm and shook his head. "No, Christopher. Sydney deserves an explanation, and no amount of apologizing will ever suffice."

"But, Dad—"

"It will be all right," Connors reassured him, and then turned back to Sydney and nodded for her to continue with her questioning.

She did so, but with a new sense of urgency, worried that there might actually be a hit team on the way to the clinic. "How were you planning on faking your death?"

"Car crash," he answered. "It's one of the classics . . . an old favorite of my late partner's, actually. After you returned with the records of my experiments"—he waved a hand toward the black bag that Sydney had set on the floor beside her—"I was going to flee with them in the Bentley.

Realizing that you had been set up, I assume that you would have given chase."

Sydney nodded ruefully; no doubt she would have done exactly as expected.

"Don't worry yourself," he said, noting the look on her face. "It would have been the right thing for you to do under the circumstances. That's the key to success in an operation like this."

His reassurances didn't make Sydney feel any better, but she chose not to dwell on it. "And what would have happened after I chased you?"

"You would have witnessed the Bentley—or, rather, *another* Bentley of the same vintage—plummeting off of a cliff not far from here and rather spectacularly exploding."

"I was kind of looking forward to that part," Christopher joked softly. "I've never seen a car explode." His father reached out and patted his hand, and Sydney—in spite of everything—was once again moved by the obvious affection between the two of them.

"Once I was dead and gone," Connors continued with a sad smile, "Christopher and May were to temporarily hand the reins of the clinic over to some of our very capable coworkers and then join me in exile on a lovely beach somewhere to help keep me company in my final few days."

Sydney was hesitant to ask the next question—chances were pretty good that she wasn't going to like the answer—and Connors sensed her unease.

"You're wondering about a body," he said, looking proud of her.

She nodded. "I assume you have one."

"I do: patient twenty-three . . . one of the shadow patients."

"Please tell me that he's already dead—and that he died of natural causes."

Again, Connors regarded her with that look of parental affection that struck Sydney as totally genuine. It was disconcerting, not least because Sloane often looked at her like that. Of course there *was* a crucial difference: With Sloane, there was something predatory—something possessive—mixed in with the affection.

Connors assured her that there was nothing untoward about patient twenty-three's demise. "He came to us during our first year in operation . . . a severely traumatized amnesiac with no family or friends to speak of, cast aside by the very people that he had sacrificed himself for. He never responded to treatment . . . although in his case that may have been a blessing. He had seen things that no man should ever see, and restoring those memories would have been cruel. Over the years, we cared for him the best we could. He grew ill last month and finally passed on, two days ago . . . when I was in Los Angeles."

"Where is the body?" Sydney asked.

"We have a small morgue in the basement of the North Wing—a necessity in this sort of clinic, I'm afraid. His body is there. I was a little uneasy about using him like this—something I wouldn't have even blinked at in the old days—but it seemed appropriate somehow: a fiery, Viking funeral for an old warrior. I try to reassure myself that he would have approved . . . but I suppose it doesn't matter now."

"So I take it that January was never actually stolen?"

"No . . . that was a complete fabrication, I'm afraid. My real fear was that someone might get ahold of it after my death—my real death—and use it as a weapon."

"Then what did my agency recover at the Leuba?"

"Tap water. British tap water, to be exact. The

arms market was to be a parting gift from the Ghost to the CIA—and, as your father no doubt surmised, an attractive piece of bait to insure their involvement in my scheme. As it turns out . . . that piece of bait was my undoing."

"The hit team?" Sydney asked, and Connors nodded in affirmation.

"Apparently, I seriously miscalculated the speed and severity with which the Leuba family would be able to retaliate for the raid. After our contact in Zurich informed us of the impending attack, I attempted to reach my friend Hopkins—the only person who could have possibly tied the raid to me and the clinic. I have not had any success reaching him and can only assume that he has given us up . . . willingly or otherwise."

Connors slumped in exhaustion. The physical and emotional strains of the past few days had finally overwhelmed him, leaving just a shell of the vibrant figure that Sydney had first encountered in Los Angeles. She felt sorry for him, but there was one last question that she needed answered.

"Why me?" she asked.

He rallied himself to sit up and look her in the eye. "The easy answer is that I needed a CIA agent to witness and confirm my death. That's the only way that my plan would work. The more difficult answer involves your father, Sydney. Like I told you before, I've kept tabs on Jack—and eventually on you—ever since that night in the jungle. Not a day goes by that I don't relive that horror . . . and I suspect that the same holds true for him. I thought that finally knowing the truth about that night—and knowing that the man responsible was dead—would help give him some sense of closure. At first I wanted to involve him more directly in my little scheme . . . but I quickly realized that it would never work."

Sydney thought about her father's reaction to Connors's presence in Los Angeles and had to agree: It would have never worked.

"And then I hit on the idea of having *you* witness my death," he continued, "and all of the pieces fell into place." He gave a rueful laugh. "In hindsight, this whole ridiculous scheme has not been my best work," he finished.

Sydney was silent for a moment, contemplating what to do next. Her father's voice in her head made it very plain what *he* would do in this situation—but he wasn't in charge here.

Her mind made up, she stood and addressed

the two men. "So . . . what do we do next? How soon is this hit team going to be here?"

Connors shook his head wearily. "Sit down, my dear. I will face the music alone. And we shall hope that they will be satisfied with having me and won't feel the need to inflict further harm on the clinic or its inhabitants."

As soon as Connors had finished speaking, Christopher launched into a loud and vehement protest. Connors was doing his best to defend his decision to his son and Sydney couldn't get a word in edgewise. Frustrated, she put two fingers in her mouth and whistled loudly—a handy skill that she had picked up at camp in sixth grade. The two men went silent and allowed her to speak.

"Listen to me. Even if I wanted to let you turn yourself over to these people—and I don't—we couldn't trust that it would satisfy them. The Leuba have a nasty reputation for overkill. These guys probably have orders to burn this place to the ground and kill anyone they find. So I suggest that we try to secure the patients and figure out some way to stop that from happening."

Connors regarded her for a moment, seeming to draw strength from her resolve. Sydney was relieved to see a little bit of the old spark returning to his eyes. "You're absolutely correct, Sydney," he said with renewed vigor. "It would be a shameful act of cowardice to leave these people at the mercy of cutthroats and miscreants. I don't know what I was thinking. If my friend's information was correct, we probably have less than an hour before the invaders arrive. Let's alert May and see what we can do about the situation."

As they were leaving the room, Christopher turned to Sydney and mouthed a silent thank-you. She nodded and followed after him into the hallway, hoping that throwing in her lot with Connors and his strange family was the right decision.

CHAPTER 23

May would have made an amazing spy, Sydney decided. She had done the lion's share of the talking on the train car and her performance had been seamless. Now she was reacting to the news that a group of men were on the way to kill Connors—and quite possibly all of them—with efficiency and a cool head.

"Right," she responded to the news, "then we need to do something about the guests immediately."

"I was thinking that we could sequester them

in the barn. It'll be cramped and cold, but if these people are going to attack us, they'll most likely concentrate on the main building," Connors suggested.

"That's fine for the ambulatory ones," May replied. "We can give them blankets, try to keep them warm and quiet . . . but there are a good dozen patients that we aren't going to be able to move that far."

"Can we at least move them to the basement?" Sydney asked. "I'm afraid that these people might try to burn us out, and I think the patients might be safer if they're off the upper floors."

May nodded. "We'll take them down to the south side of the basement. It's warm down there and—let's hope it doesn't come to this—the water from the pool might come in handy."

"An excellent idea, dear," Connors said. "We'll leave the South Wing dark and keep a few lights on in the North. It might draw the attackers' attention away for a few minutes and give us a chance to deal with the threat."

"Great. Let me assemble the staff—although I have no idea what to tell them—and I'll meet you back here in a couple of minutes." May kissed

Christopher on the cheek and hurried away, trying to think of a believable cover story.

"I'll grab Mr. Yates and get the barn ready," Christopher suggested. Connors hugged him and he ran off toward the South Wing.

"Sydney, why don't you come with me to the offices and we'll get some lights on up there."

She followed Connors to the elevators, grateful to be taking the easy route to the offices this time, and pushed the button for the third floor.

"I'm terribly sorry, Sydney," he said as the doors closed and the car started upward. "I just wanted to flex the old muscles one last time . . . go out with a bang. I never thought that anyone would get hurt . . . especially not you. I really was thrilled to finally meet you, you know."

Sydney smiled, hoping to keep his spirits up. "Well, you certainly do keep things exciting; I'll say that much for you."

"I do my best," he laughed. "Tell me," he said as they arrived on the third floor, "how was your trip over the roof? I'm sorry I didn't ask earlier."

"Under the circumstances, you're forgiven for not asking. The trip was . . . challenging," she said, still feeling the after-effects in her legs.

Connors turned on the hallway lights and unlocked several office doors as they spoke. "I made the climb myself once, just after I bought the place. 'Challenging' might be an understatement. Although there is quite a view from up there, wouldn't you say?"

He unlocked an office at the opposite end of the hallway from May's office and invited Sydney inside. It was a beautiful, wood-paneled room dominated by a massive oak desk, the top of which was completely bare, save for a telephone and a crystal vase of white roses. Sydney didn't need to wonder whose office it was.

Connors immediately set about unlocking and opening all of the drawers in the bank of sturdy filing cabinets that lined the far wall. He began removing the files and leaving them in piles on the floor. When Sydney questioned him as to why, he stopped and addressed her with complete seriousness. "If I don't leave here tonight and these people burn the clinic down, I want to make sure that these files are destroyed along with the building. I will not have anyone using my work in ways that I did not intend." She nodded and helped him empty the rest of the cabinets.

Before they left the room, Connors opened a desk drawer and removed a polished wooden box, from which he pulled a Walther PPK. He handed the gun, along with an extra magazine, to Sydney, who noted that the weapon was in beautiful condition and wondered if it was the same gun that Connors had carried in the jungle outside Nha Trang. "I can only imagine that you are more capable with one of these than I am. I never could hit a thing." She thanked him, tucked the gun into her belt, and followed him out of the room.

They left lights burning in roughly half of the offices on the third floor and then rode the elevator back to the lobby, where they were greeted by May and the rest of the clinic's live-in staff. Some of the employees appeared to still be half-asleep, but most of them were used to being roused at odd hours and were ready for action. Connors greeted them as a group and then proceeded to outline the situation.

"I'm not sure what May has already told you, but I'm afraid that we need to keep this brief." Sydney almost laughed at the idea of Connors keeping anything brief, but instead she nodded to help emphasize the seriousness of the situation as

Connors continued with his speech. "There is a group of men on their way to the clinic who wish to do us harm. This is entirely my fault and I beg your forgiveness. Ms. Bristow—as you have no doubt surmised from the firearm at her waist—is not a delusional patient, but a highly-capable expert at handling situations such as this. I know that this is all very confusing and I promise that I will explain it more thoroughly when there's time. I understand completely if any of you wish to leave now, but we could certainly use your help in making sure that our guests are safe and secure."

One of the cooks—an older woman with a thick German accent—raised her hand timidly and piped up with a question. "Is it true that they're looking for Mafia gold that Mrs. Bellomo hid on the property before she died last year?" Sydney and Connors turned to May, who gave an *I couldn't think of anything else* shrug.

Connors stifled a laugh and dispelled the Mafia gold rumor. He then asked the nurses to assist with moving the nonambulatory patients to the southern end of the basement and the other staff to help rouse the mobile guests and gather them in the barn. He sent one young man—the doctor named

Snyder who had been escorting Miss Noreen earlier in the day—to the third floor of the South Wing, telling him to keep an eye on the road from town and report any approaching vehicles. "Be sure to keep the lights off up there, Dr. Snyder—no sense drawing unwanted attention to yourself."

Sydney was impressed to note that every member of the staff stayed to help. She remained in the lobby with Connors, who had his hands full with the guests. Nearly all of them demanded—some quite angrily—to see him before they would agree to decamp to the barn. Turning on the full force of his considerable charm, Connors soothed and reassured and apologized and cajoled them into cooperating. His success rate was remarkable: Most of them wound up helping out with the evacuation and even the few remaining grumblers did as they were asked in the end.

While she was waiting for her turn to speak with Connors, the diminutive Mrs. Pearl took the opportunity to reassure Sydney that everything was going to be just fine. "Your father will take care of everything, dear. Never you worry." Connors overheard the exchange and patted Mrs. Pearl's arm affectionately.

"No need for that anymore, Mrs. Pearl. Ms. Bristow is fully aware of the fact that I'm not her father."

"She's been cured?" the tiny woman asked. Connors nodded and Mrs. Pearl's eyes widened in amazement. "That was fast," she marveled as one of the cleaning staff led her away toward the barn.

While Connors was off changing into clothes more suited for repelling, as he put it, "the invading hordes," May returned from moving a bedridden gentleman—the former president of a multibillion-dollar oil cartel—to the lower floor. She checked in with Sydney for an update on the status of the evacuation.

"Moving along," Sydney replied. "I think we have most of them either situated in the barn or on their way to it."

"Has there been any sign of—I'm not really sure what to call them—intruders, I suppose?"

"Nothing yet, but I'm afraid it won't be long now. How are you doing with the other patients?"

"I think that the last of them are on the way down," May replied, and then excused herself. "I need to round up some medical supplies for my little makeshift ward down there—and work on my poolside manner." She turned to go, then turned back to Sydney with a big smile. "By the way . . . it's nice to officially meet you, Ms. Bristow. I'm sorry that it has to be under these circumstances."

Once again Sydney was struck by May's composure. She was a remarkable woman, and she and Christopher made a lovely couple. Sydney was more convinced than ever that helping this strange little family was the right thing to do. "Call me Sydney," she replied, "and it's nice to meet you too, May."

Connors returned, now clad in black pants and sweater, just in time to help convince the final ambulatory guest—the besotted cousin of a former U.S. president—that it would be in his best interests to finish his bourbon in the barn. They had just managed to send the bleary-eyed gent on his unsteady way when Dr. Snyder came bursting through the stairwell door in a panic.

"Headlights," he panted, winded from running down three flights of stairs.

"How close?" Sydney asked, pulling Connors's gun from her belt.

"Close, I think. I saw them right as they made the turn past the stone bridge, but they must have turned off their lights after that because I didn't see them come around the next turn."

"They've probably pulled over and are coming through the woods on foot," Connors said to Sydney, then turned to the terrified doctor. "Thank you, Dr. Snyder. You've done a wonderful job. Would you mind joining May in the basement and assisting her with the patients?"

As Snyder scurried away, Christopher burst through the front doors and ran across the lobby to where Sydney and Connors were standing. "We're all set, Dad. Everyone's either in the barn or downstairs, and all of the outer doors are locked save for the front. I've killed all of the exterior lights. What should we do next?"

Connors put his hands on his son's shoulders and looked into his eyes. "Christopher, I want you to hurry back to the barn and shut yourself inside. Keep everyone calm. Sydney and I will take care of our unwanted visitors."

Christopher shook his head vigorously as he replied. "No . . . I left Nurse Burnett in charge. I'm staying with you."

Connors hugged his son tightly, but held firm in his resolve. "There's no time to argue, Son. The patients need you. Besides, Nurse Burnett will have them all singing hymns at the top of their lungs and I need you to keep them quiet. Now, listen to me very carefully. As soon as you hear something happening—no matter what it is—I want you to call the fire station in the village and get them up here. I love you, Christopher. Now go."

Realizing that his father was right, Christopher broke the hug and ran for the door, replying in kind to his father's declaration of love as he ran. "Please take care of him for me, Ms. Bristow," he shouted as he exited the building and sprinted for the barn.

When they were alone, Connors turned to Sydney and, to her surprise, drew her into his arms for a brief hug as well. A laugh escaped her lips, but she squeezed him tight for a second before pulling away. The Connors family was definitely a physically affectionate bunch. "Thank you again, Sydney," he said. "You have no idea how much this means to me." He then knelt, raised his left trouser leg, and removed a wicked-looking combat knife from a sheath strapped to his calf. "Shall we?" he asked, sounding just like he was inviting her onto a dance floor.

CHAPTER 24

Sydney and Connors locked the front door behind them and then sprinted across the lawn for a clump of bushes, just to the left of the front gates. It would provide them with cover and a view of the main building and the barn. Sydney was impressed with how quickly Connors moved. The adrenaline rush of the past hour seemed to be doing wonders for him.

They reached the bushes and crouched behind them, catching their breath and letting their eyes adjust to the darkness. Sydney looked back across the lawn they had just crossed and took stock of the situation. She had Connors's pistol—six shots in the magazine, plus one in the barrel and a further six in the spare mag—and Connors had his knife. They were only two—a highly capable expert with very sore legs, and a dying old man—against who knew how many. Their only advantage, as far she could tell, was the fact that the strike team wouldn't know that they were expected, and that she and Connors knew the layout of the grounds.

They were just inside the fence line to the north of the gates and she could see the entire front of the main building from their vantage point. To the left, past the South Wing, she could just make out the shape of the barn. She knew that the greenhouse lay to the right of the main building, beyond the rose garden, but without the benefit of moonlight, she couldn't see it at all. The lights from the offices in the North Wing stood out like a beacon in the inky darkness but didn't cast much light onto the grounds themselves.

It was Connors's contention that the attack, when it came, would most likely be from the woods that lay to the north, past the greenhouse. Now all they could do was wait for it.

They didn't have to wait long. A fireball came screaming across the night sky—from the woods, as expected—and slammed into the top floor of the North Wing. The rocket exploded and blew out the windows on the entire floor. The sound of glass raining down on the paved walkways surrounding the building was followed by a few seconds of eerie silence, during which the flickering orange light of multiple fires began to glow in the upper offices.

The sibilant hiss of the sprinkler system turning on and raining water on flame was followed closely by the shriek of another rocket, this one striking the middle floor and causing a large section of the north end of the clinic to collapse. The flames grew higher, overwhelming the sprinklers, and began to spread.

"We've got half an hour until the fire crew gets here," Connors whispered tersely. "What do you say you and I make sure that there's no one left shooting by the time they arrive?" Sydney nodded and followed Connors as he broke cover and sprinted along the fence line to their right, hoping to flank their unseen attackers.

As they crested a hillock about fifty yards from their original position, Connors came to a sudden stop and dropped to the ground. Sydney followed suit, taking up a prone position beside him, facing the rose garden. Connors gestured toward the hedges ringing the garden and Sydney could just make out two shadowy figures—barely illuminated by the orange glow of the flames—creeping toward the clinic, automatic assault rifles at the ready. There were no other intruders in sight.

"The others must be circling around back," Connors whispered. "Why don't we try to retain the element of surprise for as long as possible and take these two out quietly?" Sydney agreed, and again followed Connors's lead.

They crept down the sloping mound—keeping low and sticking to the shadows—toward their unsuspecting prey. The two men were so focused on the main building, ready to gun down anyone who fled the burning structure, that Sydney and Connors were able to get within feet of them before attacking.

Connors held up his hand, motioning for Sydney to stand still, and then lunged for the two men before she could even react.

With surprising speed and economy of movement, Connors wrapped his left arm around the head of the man on the left, pulled it back, and drew his blade across the man's exposed throat with his right hand. He let the man go and continued with his motion to the right, pivoting and plunging his knife into the chest of the other man. His aim was perfect—the blade slid in between the fifth and sixth ribs and pierced the heart. It was over in just a few seconds. The first man never even knew what hit him and dropped without a sound. The second man's finger jerked convulsively when Connors stabbed him and he fired a single shot that streaked harmlessly into the sky as he died.

Sydney stared at Connors in openmouthed amazement. The only other time she had seen someone dispatch multiple adversaries with such efficiency, it had been her father wielding the knife. Connors shrugged, looking almost embarrassed by what he'd just done. "After Nha Trang," he said quietly, "I took some lessons."

"No kidding," she replied as they stripped the corpses of their weapons and ammunition.

Connors rolled the bodies over in order to get a better look at the men that he had ushered into the afterlife. Sydney had been worried that they were up against a well-trained hit squad or even foreign intelligence agents, but these men didn't have that polished, professional look about them. "Mercenaries, I'd guess," Connors said, noting the leathery, weathered faces common to men that have spent most of their lives outdoors in the war-torn regions of the world. "That's good. They'll probably just blunder around, blowing things up. Makes them easy to spot."

As if in response to his remark, an explosion rocked the center section of the main building. The lower windows were blown outward, spraying glass across the front lawn. The enormous panes in the ceiling cracked with a sound like thunder and then collapsed inward. The noise was deafening. "We need to stop them before they target the South Wing, the bastards," Connors growled, then succumbed to a coughing fit.

Sydney was worried that the exertions of the evening were catching up to him again and that she would be left to defend the clinic alone. "Why don't I run around . . . try to get behind and drive them toward you?" she suggested. She hoped that her strategy would give Connors a chance to catch his breath.

He was struggling to stifle his coughing, worried

that the noise would draw unwanted attention, but he managed to nod his approval of her suggestion. He gestured for her to head for the south end of the building and indicated that he would try to circle around north. She clapped him on the arm in support, and then took off running across the lawn. She had tucked the pistol in her belt again and was carrying one of the fallen merc's AK-47s.

She ran toward the South Wing, hoping that she could make it around the far end of the building in time to drive the attackers back the way they had come—just in case any of them were moving toward the barn. *They'll be wondering why no one has fled the building yet . . . trying to figure out where everyone went.* As she ran, she wondered about the people huddled together in the barn and the basement. *Those poor people must be terrified,* she thought, and pushed herself to run faster.

As she rounded the south end of the building, she caught sight of two more mercenaries, stalking across the rear lawns toward the barn. One of the men was carrying a rifle in the ready position—braced against his shoulder, finger on the trigger—but the other was equipped with what appeared to be a shoulder-fired rocket launcher.

Sydney watched in horror as the man with the rocket launcher knelt on the ground and raised the weapon to his shoulder—pointing it directly at the barn. She skidded to a stop and raised her purloined assault rifle to firing position, sighted on the man with the rocket, and squeezed off two quick shots. The man collapsed, falling to one side, but managed to pull the trigger as he fell. Sydney gasped, her heart leaping into her throat, as a plume of flame shot from the back end of the weapon and the small projectile on the front streaked away toward the barn. She breathed a sigh of relief as the shot went wide—barely missing the barn and continuing on to explode in the air over the dark waters of Lake Lucerne.

Sydney dropped to the ground as the other mercenary spun in her direction and opened fire, spraying bullets wildly in an attempt to hit a target he couldn't see. She lined up a shot and took him down with one well-placed round.

In the distance, Sydney could hear the wail of a fire engine's siren approaching. She got to her feet and ran for the back corner of the building. The element of surprise was no longer an issue—she needed to find a secure position and take out as many of these guys as possible before the fire crew arrived.

She hoped that the man she just killed was the only one equipped with a rocket launcher, but her hopes were dashed by the telltale shrieking noise of a rocket followed by the inevitable explosion. This blast was farther away than the others and Sydney guessed that the greenhouse was going to be in serious need of repairs.

Sydney reached the corner of the building and risked a peek around the edge. She could see the greenhouse burning in the distance, as expected, but that was the least of her troubles. Four more mercenaries—silhouetted against the flames—were advancing toward her. Hopefully this was the remainder of the attack force. They had fanned out across the rear lawn—three with the familiar Russian-made assault rifles, ready to fire, while the fourth was carrying another rocket launcher.

She dropped to one knee and sighted down the barrel of the rifle at the merc with the rocket launcher. She would be giving away her position, but it was more important to take out the man with the big firepower. Two quick shots and the mercenaries' numbers dropped to three.

The remaining attackers instantly scrambled for cover and unleashed a barrage of well-placed gunfire, forcing Sydney to duck back behind the corner. The three men worked efficiently, keeping Sydney pinned behind the wall while they advanced toward the southern edge of the building.

The south lawn was an unbroken expanse of grass, running all the way to the barn, which offered no cover at all. When the mercenaries reached the edge of the building—which they would in just seconds—Sydney was going to be completely exposed. She thought about running back toward the front of the building, but she knew that she'd never make it in time. She could shoot the lock on the side door to the clinic and hide inside, but she didn't want to draw the attacker's attention back to the South Wing. She scooted backward from the corner and lay prone on the ground next to the wall, hoping that she would be harder to spot. She raised the rifle, sighted on the corner, and waited.

One of the mercenaries darted across the back lawn and dove behind a large wooden planter, about thirty feet from the back wall. Sydney's finger tensed on the trigger, but she refrained from firing. She didn't want to give away her position for the sake of a risky shot.

The man behind the planter was now in a position to view the south wall. Sydney remained perfectly still. She didn't think that he'd be able to see her until she moved or fired her weapon. The merc sprayed the lawn to Sydney's left with a stream of bullets, hoping to draw her out. Her heart was racing, but she didn't have a clear shot and refrained from returning fire.

A second merc poked his head around the corner and then ducked back, again trying to bait her into firing and giving up her position. She was going to have to do something soon—before she became vulnerable to all three remaining attackers. She gritted her teeth and aimed for the corner of the building, hoping the second merc would risk another peek. But she was saved from having to reveal herself by a familiar voice, shouting from the rear of the clinic.

"Are you looking for me?" Connors's voice rang out, followed by a burst of gunfire. The merc behind the planter screamed and fell to the ground. The odds were now even.

Sydney couldn't see Connors, but she assumed

he must have made his way around the north end of the building and surprised their attackers from behind. She could hear gunfire from the two remaining mercs and took advantage of their distraction to sprint across the lawn, trying to reach a position from which she could help Connors.

She reached the bodies of the two men she killed earlier and dove to the ground behind them, using their corpses to shield her—as much as possible—from the eyes and bullets of the two remaining gunmen.

From this angle, she could tell that Connors was holed up inside the clinic and realized that he must have braved the flames and wreckage in the lobby and cut straight through the building. She could see the muzzle flash from his rifle, returning fire at the two surviving mercs, who were keeping him pinned down with a steady barrage.

She had a clear view of one of the two men and rose to her elbows so that she could line up a shot. Just as she was about to pull the trigger, she saw something fly through the air and into the lobby.

"Connors! *Grenade!*" she yelled, drawing the attention of the gunman she had been about to shoot. He rolled to the side—out of her line of fire—just as the grenade his partner had thrown exploded in the lobby, throwing glass and shrapnel across most of the rear courtyard.

The blast was followed by a loud cry from behind Sydney. "Dad!" Christopher screamed and came sprinting across the lawn from the direction of the barn. Sydney realized that he must have sneaked out of hiding and had been watching the unfolding events from a distance.

"Christopher, GET DOWN!" she yelled to him as the remaining mercenaries opened fire in their direction. A bullet slammed into Christopher's thigh and he went down with a cry.

Sydney rose to her feet, spraying bullets in the direction of the two men, hoping to keep them pinned down long enough to reach Christopher. If he was able to move, she would try to provide cover fire while he hobbled to a safer position. And if he wasn't able to move . . . *I'll just have to improvise,* she thought grimly.

Just as she reached Christopher's side, the smoking rifle in her hands locked up and quit firing. *What the hell? AK's never jam,* she thought, and hit the ground beside Christopher, reaching for the pistol in her belt—but it was gone. She knew it must have fallen while she was running. "Have you got a weapon?" she asked Christopher.

"No," he replied as a line of bullets stitched the ground not five feet in front of them. "I'm sorry, Sydney," he said with the resigned tone of someone who knew that all was lost.

The grenade had exploded directly in front of Connors's position and nothing had been heard from him since. They had to assume the worst. Sydney could hear the fire engines turning into the drive in front of the clinic. The two mercenaries had risen to their feet and were advancing toward them cautiously—wanting to get a better shot, but afraid that they might be walking into a trap. She could only see one option.

"Play dead," she whispered to Christopher. "I'm going to try to draw their fire. If they chase me, get up and move as fast as you can away from here. Don't let them see you. Good luck, Christopher."

Before he could protest, she rolled to the side and rose to her feet, moving faster than she would have thought possible. She heard a volley of gunfire and dove for the ground, tucking her right shoulder down so that she could roll forward and keep running. Bullets whistled past her head—far too close for comfort—but didn't find their target. She pumped her aching legs as hard as she ever had, trying to outrun the inevitable.

Another round of gunfire followed, immediately answered by a new sound: the distinctive flat-sounding *pop* of a .45 automatic—two .45s, actually—being discharged. She dove for the ground again but stayed down this time. She rolled to a stop and looked back toward the clinic . . . and one of the most welcome sights she had ever seen.

Jack Bristow—in black tactical gear, a blazing pistol in either hand—was charging around the south end of the clinic and into the rear courtyard. He had already dispatched the nearest gunman and was bearing down on the second one. The man rose from his position behind an overturned wooden table and swung his rifle toward Jack, but he never had a chance. Without slowing up a bit, Jack trained both guns on the man and emptied his remaining rounds into the mercenary's chest.

Jack paused only to eject the spent magazines from his guns and pop new ones into place before hurrying across the lawn to where Sydney was just rising to her feet. He tucked the guns into his belt, grabbed his daughter without a word, and pulled her into his arms.

Jack hugged Sydney as if his life depended on it, but only for a moment. "Was that the last of them?" he asked urgently, pulling away from her.

She nodded. "I think so."

"Where is Connors?"

"Dad, he's dead—," she began to reply, but Jack cut her off.

"Where?" he demanded.

She pointed toward the demolished center section of the clinic. "He was in there, but—" Jack was already on the move, running for the back of the clinic. "Dad, *don't!*" she screamed—but nothing could stop Jack. She saw him enter the back of the burning building, guns drawn.

Realizing that there was nothing she could do for Connors or her father, Sydney turned her attention to other matters. "Christopher . . . are you okay?" she called out as she stooped to retrieve a pistol from one of the fallen mercs.

"I'm fine," he yelled to her, "but we need to get May and the patients out of the basement."

Sydney was already running full speed toward

the south side door of the clinic. "I'm on it," she called over her shoulder.

She fired two shots into the locked door handle and then gave it a well-placed kick. The door flew open with a crash. Sydney stepped inside the darkened hallway and felt along the wall for a light switch. The overhead lights blinked on and Sydney breathed a sigh of relief. Still having power in this wing would make getting the patients out a lot easier.

Thin ribbons of smoke were beginning to filter in from the fires in the other parts of the building. She ran to the far end of the hallway and pressed the button to call the elevator. She heard the machinery kick in, raising the car from the level below. When it arrived, Sydney got in and rode to the basement. The doors chimed and slid open and Sydney found herself face-to-face with May—who was brandishing a fire ax over her head.

"May, it's me. . . . It's Sydney," she yelled, stopping the downward stroke.

"Sydney! Thank God," May gasped. "Is it over?"

Sydney nodded. "It's over . . . but we need to get everyone out of here quickly."

Without hesitation, May threw herself into organizing her second evacuation of the evening. Only when things were proceeding efficiently and the immediate danger had passed, did she take a moment to voice the question that she was dying to ask.

"Is Christopher . . . ," she began, but couldn't bring herself to finish the sentence.

"He's fine," Sydney reassured her.

"And Dr. Connors?"

Sydney didn't answer out loud, just shook her head sadly. May nodded, and then turned back to the job at hand.

Ten in the morning and it was all over. Most of the clinic was a smoldering ruin . . . although the South Wing had remained virtually untouched. Many of the guests had already been shuttled to hotels—and hospitals, where appropriate—and the exhausted fire crew was starting to pack up their equipment. The cousin of the former president staggered around, regaling anyone who would listen with tales of his heroism. A team of police inspectors had been helicoptered in and were taking charge of the bodies of the mercenaries.

Sydney sat on the tailgate of a pickup truck—a local tavern had used it to deliver coffee and pastries for the fire crew—that was parked in the middle of the front lawn and watched the bustle of activity around her.

She watched as May and Christopher, whose wounded leg was wrapped in a pristine white bandage, helped to load the last of the patients into an ambulance and sent it on its way. They stood in silence for a moment, surveying the wreckage of the clinic and their lives, then wrapped their arms around each other and wept.

Sydney turned away from the heartbreaking sight and scanned the area for her father. She saw him talking to the unhappy head of the police team, who had just been informed by his superiors that Jack and Sydney were not to be detained.

Jack finished up with the police and came walking across the lawn to the pickup. He sat down on the tailgate, next to Sydney, and waited for her to speak.

It had taken Sydney a while to find Jack after she emerged from the basement with May. She had searched for him frantically, terrified that he had been trapped in the burning building. It was only after the sun had risen and the fire had been mostly contained that she had seen him walking up the main drive from the road. His face and clothes had been covered in soot and ash. And his hands were red with blood.

Something in Jack's eyes—an almost unbearable sadness—had prevented her from asking him what had happened at the time. But now he seemed ready to talk.

"Can you tell me about it?" she asked quietly.

He cleared his throat, and then spoke in a low, calm voice. "There isn't too much to tell. I found him just inside the back doors to the lobby. The grenade must have killed him."

"What about the blood, Dad? Why was there blood on your hands?"

Jack looked ashamed, but he answered her question. "I had to be sure. He was facedown when I found him. I had to turn him over and see his face. I just had to be sure this time."

Sydney nodded her head in understanding but didn't say anything, so Jack continued. "Afterward, I had to clear my head. I walked down the road for a while, and then walked back. I'm sorry, sweetheart. I didn't mean to worry you."

"Is it all over now?" she asked, looking across the lawn toward Christopher and May.

Jack followed her gaze to the grieving couple, and then turned quickly away. "Yes," he said simply, "it's all over. Let's go home."

CHAPTER 25

VIETNAM, 1971

Connors knew that his friend was about to kill him. The experiment had worked—far too well, in fact—and the situation was completely out of control.

"Come here, Peterson," Jack said, brandishing the knife that still dripped with Hutchins's blood. There was a smile on Jack's face that chilled Connors to the bone—his unwitting test subject was enjoying this now.

Connors was pointing his gun at Jack, hoping that the sight of it would be enough to deter his friend from attacking. The last thing on earth that

Connors wanted to do was shoot the young man that he had grown so close to over the past few days, but he might not have a choice. He considered telling Jack his real name, but decided that it would probably just confuse and enrage the man further. "Jack . . . I need you to listen. You have to stay calm. I'm not going to hurt you . . . and I know that you don't really want to hurt me."

"Are you sure about that?" Jack said, and laughed—a horrible, cackling noise, the likes of which Connors had never heard before. "Because I think I do want to hurt you."

Jack was slowly but steadily advancing as he spoke. He seemed to be toying with Connors, making a game out of it. He didn't seem the least bit afraid of the gun.

Connors was out of time and needed to act. He knew that if he could get Jack's heart rate up, it would speed the body's absorption of the drug. It might mean that the effects would intensify for a while, but they would also run their course sooner. Connors knew that he couldn't outrun Jack—especially not now that the drug was rendering the man more or less impervious to pain and fear—and he needed to gain whatever advantage he could. "I'm sorry, Jack," he said. Then he dropped his aim and fired a shot into Jack's left leg.

The bullet struck just above the knee and Jack howled like an animal in pain. Connors didn't even hesitate after pulling the trigger—he turned and ran as fast as his legs could carry him.

Connors had only the vaguest idea of which way to head. He had triggered the radio beacon as soon as the first scream had awakened them, and he had to trust that the extraction team—who had been on twenty-four hour alert—would be on their way. They were to rendezvous at the remnants of Nguyen Quang's compound, which lay a short distance—no more than a few kilometers—to the east of the ruined temple. Connors was fairly sure he knew which direction was east, but there was no time to check the compass, and dawn was still a few hours off.

Behind him, crashing through the jungle like a wild boar, Connors could hear Jack hobbling after him. Jack was moving fast, and Connors worried that his friend might be losing a lot of blood. Ideally, if and when they made it to the extraction point, the drug would have worn off enough to let Jack gain some control over his actions—but none of that would matter if he bled to death on the way. The trick for Connors was going to be staying far enough ahead of Jack so that he couldn't catch up, but not so far ahead that he might lose the trail and get lost in the jungle.

Connors soon realized that he didn't need to worry about getting too far in front of Jack. With a terrifying roar, Jack poured on a burst of speed and came within inches of catching up to his quarry. Connors cut left sharply and vaulted a downed tree trunk, silently urging his aching legs to move faster. Jack tried to corner and his wounded leg buckled underneath him. A bone cracked as he fell, but he didn't slow down for a second. He scrambled to his feet and set off after Connors again.

They ran for what seemed like hours to Connors. He was fast over short distances, but he had never been a distance runner and his legs and lungs were burning. Jack had been slowed down by the fall and the broken bone, but he was beginning to gain again. Just as Connors was making a silent vow to give up the cigars if he made it out of the jungle, he burst out of the brush into a small clearing. He stumbled over the stones of an abandoned fire pit and fell face-first to the ground. The wind was knocked out of him and the Walther was torn from his grip by the impact. Connors heard it clatter away across the rocky ground. They had reached Quang's abandoned compound.

Connors had just struggled to his feet when Jack arrived. He could see that Jack was in bad shape. His face was pale and his left ankle looked like it was bent too far to the side. Connors could see the blood on Jack's pant leg, shining in the moonlight, and hoped that the extraction team arrived soon.

The two men stared at each other for a few seconds. Jack seemed to be struggling against the rage that had gripped him, and Connors was grateful for the opportunity to catch his breath.

When he had recovered enough to speak, Connors tried to reason with his friend. "The extraction team is on the way, Jack. Everything is going to be okay. You just need to stay calm. We'll get your leg fixed up and you'll be right as rain."

The mention of his leg seemed to enrage Jack, overriding what little control he had regained. Once again, he lunged forward, knife in hand.

Connors tried to run, but he was too slow. Jack managed to grab the back of Connors's sweater with his free hand. He spun Connors around and plunged his knife into the man's chest. He quickly pulled the knife out—and then drove it in again.

Jack let go of Connors and let him fall to the ground, the handle of the knife sticking out of his chest. The act of stabbing this man who had been his friend shocked him to his senses for a moment. "Peterson?" he inquired, afraid that no answer would be forthcoming.

Connors groaned and tried to sit up. He could just barely make out Jack's face in the moonlight. The man looked like he was struggling against an irresistible force.

"Fight it, Jack," Connors gasped, struggling to speak.

"Peterson . . . what's happening to me?" Jack could feel another wave of rage building behind his eyes, his vision beginning to turn red. "I'm sorry, Peterson. I don't think I can stop it."

Connors was desperately clutching at straws. He knew he wouldn't survive another attack. He needed to find some way to channel Jack's aggression.

"King's pawn to E-four," he croaked out. Jack looked confused, so Connors repeated himself.

"King's pawn to E-four, Jack. It's your turn."

Jack managed to respond, his face contorting with the effort. "Pawn . . . to . . . C-five," he rasped.

Without the slightest pause, Connors shot back with his move. "Knight to F-three—your move, Jack."

A wave of fury washed over Jack. He fought against it, focusing all of his concentration on the game board. He practically screamed his response. "Pawn to D-six."

Again and again, Connors barked out his moves and then demanded that Jack respond. There was no thought of winning or losing for Connors—he just needed to keep Jack focused. For his part, Jack seemed to understand instinctively what Connors was doing and played more and more aggressively—channeling all of his rage into the game.

After a few minutes, Jack blundered into a checkmate. Connors didn't even give him time to think about it.

"Pawn to D-four . . . go!" he demanded with all the energy he could muster. In the distance, Connors could hear the thumping of an approaching helicopter. All he had to do was hold on until they arrived—but he felt himself growing lightheaded.

They made it through a second quick game, but Connors was finished. His vision blurred and he knew that he couldn't continue. As he was losing consciousness, Connors saw Jack—his face still contorted with the internal fight against the drug—reaching down for the knife that was still embedded in Connors's chest.

When Connors awoke, the first thing he saw was Jack Bristow, sitting in a chair by the foot of his bed, reading a book. Jack's left leg was in a cast, and the back of his head was bandaged, but he didn't look too bad—considering what he'd been through. Connors, on the other hand, felt as if he'd been through the wringer and imagined he probably looked it, too. His chest ached, but the pain felt dull and far away. He realized that he was feeling the effects of a painkiller—morphine, most likely—and tried to imagine how bad that ache would be without the benefit of drugs. There was a drip in his left arm and Connors wondered how long he'd been in the hospital.

He lay still for a moment, thinking about those

last few hours in the jungle and wondering if Jack was present in a friendly capacity or not. Deciding that there was no sense in delaying the inevitable, Connors cleared his throat.

Jack looked up and saw that the man in the bed was awake. He closed the book and set it aside, his eyes never leaving Connors's. After a long silence, he finally spoke. "They tell me your name is actually Connors," he said, his voice betraying nothing of his thoughts.

Connors tried to affirm that yes, that was indeed his name, but his throat was too dry for him to even make a sound. He nodded his head.

Jack rose from the chair and limped to the bedside table, where he poured a glass of water from a pitcher and offered it to Connors, thoughtfully providing a drinking straw as well. Once Connors had drunk his fill, Jack set aside the glass and pulled his chair up to the side of the bed so that they could speak more privately.

Connors glanced around the room while Jack was moving the chair. It was a long, narrow hospital ward, with a row of beds down either side. Bright sunlight was streaming through open windows with billowing white curtains, set along the walls above the beds. Through the windows he could hear the traffic noise and bustle of a major city, and assumed they must be in Saigon.

It took a while for Jack to speak again, and Connors didn't want to say anything until he knew his friend's state of mind. It wasn't hard to imagine that Jack might want to take revenge on Connors for what had happened.

"You saved my life," Jack began simply. "It would have been a lot simpler for you just to shoot me. Thank you."

Connors breathed a slight sigh of relief—apparently Jack wasn't here seeking revenge. "How long have I been here?"

"Almost three days," Jack answered.

Connors nodded, thinking about that last night in the jungle—and what kind of man would actually be able to *thank* him after what happened. His guilt was almost overwhelming. "Jack . . . your life would never have been in danger, had it not been for me. So, thank *you*. I saw how hard you were fighting against the drug. You're a good man. And you didn't deserve to be put through that. I'm sorry."

Waving off the apology, Jack questioned

Connors about the nature of the drug. "I understand that you slipped it to me in the chocolate bar—I figured that much out, although I could have sworn you ate it too—but what kind of compound was it? The effects were"—Jack struggled for the right words—"they were extraordinary," he concluded, in characteristically reserved Jack Bristow fashion.

"I call it Janus Twenty-three," Connors replied, "and as the name would indicate, it has been in the works for quite a while."

Connors filled Jack in on the history of his research. He told him all about the process of developing the drug that was used in the jungle—and the harrowing results of testing the substance on himself and his assistants. He surprised Jack with the revelation that, like its mythological namesake, Janus Twenty-three had two faces. There were actually two substances that worked in tandem: the primary drug—delivered in the chocolate, as Jack had surmised—and a triggering agent that was inhaled with the smoke from Connors's cigars. He related how he had discovered that one of the drug-laced chocolate bars had gone missing on that night in the jungle, and he reasoned that

Hutchins had swiped it and shared it with Martin and Lewis—throwing off the intended effects of the experiment with disastrous consequences. He showed Jack the simple magic trick he had used to palm the tainted chocolate in order to avoid consuming it himself. And he shared with Jack his vision of a whole new kind of espionage, based on game theory, psychological manipulation, and the strategic use of chemicals like Janus.

"Judging from the way things went on the mission," Jack responded, "I'd say you could use an extra hand next time you attempt something like that." It was clear that Jack was willing to be that extra hand.

Connors was amazed, and happily so. He accepted Jack's tacit offer with a nod.

"But we need to clarify something," Jack continued. "We will not be having a repeat of this disaster. I was responsible for the lives of those boys, and I am going to have to deal with that. I will not have any more innocent blood on my hands."

Connors hung his head in shame. "Their deaths will haunt me for the rest of my life," he said.

"Then we're agreed?" Jack continued. "There will be no more unwilling experimentation on our own men?"

"Agreed," Connors said, and shook Jack's outstretched hand.

"I suppose I should let you rest," Jack said, rising from the chair. "Unless of course you were feeling up to a game?" he asked.

Connors smiled. "I'd love to, but I'm afraid I don't quite remember the outcome of the last match."

"In that case, I definitely won," Jack laughed, and then settled back into his chair for the game. "Let's see now—pawn to F-four, I think."

CHAPTER 26

LOS ANGELES

"How can you stay inside on such an amazingly beautiful day?" Sydney was giving Vaughn a hard time about wanting to remain in bed for another hour—even though it was eight in the morning on a Sunday and she probably could have used some extra sleep herself. "Don't you want to come for a jog with me and then go out to breakfast?" she asked, pulling down the blanket and playfully biting him on the shoulder.

"Ow," he protested, "be careful. I'm still wounded." Vaughn pulled the blanket back up and burrowed his head underneath the pillow, trying not to laugh.

"You're a big faker . . . and you've been milking this supposed injury for long enough," she said, and attempted to pull the blanket back down. He managed to hold on to the blanket, but lost the battle against laughing.

"I'm not faking it," he declared when the laughter had subsided enough for him to talk. "You weren't there. You have no idea how big this guy was. He was like the Mount Everest of bodyguards. Ask Nadia . . . she'll tell you."

"I did ask Nadia. She said he wasn't all that big. Way more Hollywood Hills than Mount Everest."

"It's not true . . . he was Everest. You can ask Weiss. Nadia is just lying because she's mad that her boyfriend looks better in chaps than she does."

"Nadia told me all about your little trip to Mexico. She said a real little guy beat you all up first . . . in some hotel room."

"He beat up Weiss and Dixon. I'm the one who finally knocked him out."

She whistled, impressed. "Wow . . . you knocked him out? Cool. Whose hotel room was that, by the way?"

Vaughn groaned and burrowed deeper—

apparently he was never going to live this down.

"I suppose you think that I don't know what you're doing?" Sydney continued. "You just want to lie around in bed all day and dream about your hot little friend. What was her name again? Marta? Is that it? Are you just going to lie around all day, dreaming about hot Marta?"

"Believe me, I'm definitely not dreaming about hot Marta. Hot Marta scared the hell out of me." Vaughn desperately wanted to change the topic. "Just one more hour," he begged, "and then I'll take hot Sydney out to breakfast."

"Promise?"

"I promise. Cross my heart, and all that stuff," he mumbled.

"Okay," she said as she pulled on her running shoes. "But you know what happens if you break a promise, don't you?"

He sighed—there was no escaping it. "Baby gets spanked?" he asked with weary resignation.

"That's right. Baby gets spanked," she laughed, and headed for the door.

It really was a beautiful morning, the most beautiful she'd seen since her trip to the farmer's market the week before. She jogged along the boardwalk—which was already thick with tourists and street vendors—and thought about the events of the past few days.

The flight back from Zurich had been quiet. Jack was still preoccupied with his own thoughts and Sydney took the opportunity to catch up on the sleep that she had been missing.

Back in Los Angeles she had been debriefed by Sloane—never her favorite activity—and then locked herself away for two days with Vaughn . . . helping him "recuperate." Nadia had stayed over at Eric's in order to give them some time alone.

When Sydney returned to the office two days later, she was curious to hear if there had been any fallout from the events in Switzerland. The international press had been full of lurid reports of a failed robbery attempt at the Devereaux that had resulted in a terrible fire. According to the papers, the clinic had been destroyed, but the robbery had been foiled by a certain brave cousin of a former U.S. president. There was nothing in the papers about the death of the clinic's founder.

Sydney was able to ascertain that the Devereaux had been closed down for good—hardly surprising, considering the shape it had been in—and the patients relocated to other facilities. There had been some grumbling about potential lawsuits but—perhaps realizing the unwanted publicity that such undertakings would attract—no one seemed eager to actually go through with one. She had tried to get in touch with Christopher and May, but they seemed to have vanished.

Sloane had informed her that the wreckage of the clinic was still being searched, but that Connors's body had been recovered—only identifiable by the Janus-head ring on his finger. He went on to say that an autopsy had been performed, and that Jack had requisitioned a copy of the coroner's report. Sydney's heart sank when she heard that.

"I thought he was over it," she'd said sadly. "Did he say what he planned to do with it?"

"He didn't have to," Sloane had answered. "Your father took the report and flew to Washington. He spent the last two days combing through CIA archives and finally came up with a misfiled binder containing Connors's old dental records. The teeth were a match for the autopsy. I think that he has laid the Ghost to rest once and for all."

"What about the clinic?" she asked. "Were Connors's files destroyed?"

"Completely," Sloane answered. "Almost nothing remained of the North Wing once they finally got the fires out. They're still looking, but it seems unlikely that anything survived. No one will be able to use Connors's work for any purpose, noble or otherwise, now."

Life had returned to normal—as normal as it could ever be for Sydney. She and Nadia had finally spent an afternoon together and Sydney got the scoop on the Mexico City mission. "So much good blackmail material," she had lamented. "I can't believe I missed it."

Her father had returned from Washington, looking like himself again. He seemed to be in an uncommonly good mood by Jack Bristow standards. He brought Marshall a new test tube rack to replace the one that he had smashed, and had even gone out for dinner with Sydney *and* Vaughn—a rare occurrence indeed. The haunted look was gone from his eyes, and Sydney hoped that the terrors of Nha Trang were finally behind him.

And now she was going to spend a wonderful

day with the man she loved and then fly to Berlin this evening to steal the plans for a prototype suitcase bomb that had a previously unimagined capacity for destruction. All in all just another typical day at the office.

As she jogged past the pier, with its arcades and carnival rides, she thought about Connors. It seemed to Sydney, in retrospect, that Connors had wanted to tell the truth all along—but he had grown so accustomed to lies and deception that he had been rendered incapable of completely setting them aside. She thought about their time together, reliving their conversations on the train and in the clinic, and was amazed to realize that most of what he said *had* been true—he just felt the need to conceal that truth within an elaborate ruse. But she couldn't judge him too harshly. In the end, she believed, he *had* been a good man with a genuine desire to make up for the wrongs that he had done.

And then she thought about her father, and his inability to forgive Connors for the horrors in the jungle. And she thought about Sloane, and her own inability to forgive him. Even if Sloane's reformation was genuine—and Sydney had nothing but doubts as to that—there was no going back for her.

She tolerated Sloane, for Nadia's sake, but she would never forgive him for what he had taken from her.

She reflected on this unwillingness to forgive for a while, and decided that she could live with it. It helped her to understand her father and his recent behavior a little better—although it disturbed her just a little bit to think that this understanding was based on a mutual capacity for undying hatred.

She had reached the end of the jogging path. Shaking her head clear of troubling thoughts, she turned around and headed back toward her house, looking forward to breakfast. Or getting to spank Vaughn. Either one worked for her.

Sydney sprinted the final quarter mile and, once she reached her front porch, stopped to catch her breath. She bent forward at the waist and grabbed the backs of her calves, stretching her legs to avoid cramping. As she straightened up, her eye fell on something resting on the middle of three steps leading to her porch: a single white rose.

Her blood ran cold. Immediately she ran through a hundred increasingly bizarre explanations in her mind, trying to make some sense out of the situation. She knew that she had to alert APO and let Sloane know that Connors might still be alive. If he was, that meant that January might still be out there—and still a threat. And she should probably tell her father that the dental records had been faked, that he had most likely discovered the planted records of patient twenty-three. She hated to do it to him—he had been so happy for the past few days—but it was important that he know. And speaking of patient twenty-three, wouldn't he still have been in the clinic's morgue? She wondered if the team combing through the ruins of the Devereaux clinic had come across any other bodies. Sydney was willing to bet that they hadn't.

"Would you mind not picking roses from my yard?" The shrill voice of her next-door neighbor, the dreaded Mr. Falb, interrupted her thoughts. She turned to see him peering out at her from behind his rose bushes—his *white* rose bushes.

"I didn't pick it," she stammered. "It was just lying here. Probably just the wind blew it across, or maybe a cat . . . or . . . a squirrel carried it." She silently cursed the complete and utter lameness of that explanation.

"Do animals frequently bring you flowers?" he

asked in the snottiest tone imaginable—Sydney could hardly blame him.

She ran through a quick checklist of potential smart-ass replies, but realized that the satisfaction that using one of them provided would be fleeting compared to the hassle of being at war with the neighbor. "I'm sorry, Mr. Falb," she called out sweetly. "It won't happen again."

He walked away in a huff, leaving her standing there drenched in sweat and holding a white rose.

She looked at the flower and thought about Connors and smiled sadly. It might not have been a cat or a squirrel that had left the rose for her—but it was even less likely to have been a Ghost.

EPILOGUE

BRAZIL, THREE MONTHS LATER

The full moon had risen and, from where Jack Bristow was standing, was perfectly positioned behind the head of the enormous statue known as Christ the Redeemer, giving it the appearance of a halo in a medieval painting. The statue stood, with arms outstretched, at the top of the Corcovado mountain in the middle of Rio de Janeiro—and Jack stood at the statue's base, waiting for his contact.

It was supposed to be a simple transfer. Jack was to hand over a suitcase full of money, and his contact—a sleazy thief and assassin named Zé Maravilhosa, who had done some work for SD-6 many years ago—was to come across with a computer disk containing the complete roster of a large terrorist organization with cells all across South America.

Zé, or "Marvelous Joe," as he was known, had contacted Jack using an old e-mail address and suggested that he had certain valuable information that he would be willing to part with for a price. Jack had replied to the message, listened to Zé's sales pitch, and then duly passed the information along to Sloane, washing his own hands of the matter.

It was an easy mission—not the kind of thing with which Jack would normally concern himself. So Sloane was surprised when Jack came to him the next day—after reading the morning papers—and said that he wanted to handle the transfer himself. When Sloane questioned his motivations, Jack had been uncharacteristically vague. "It's just a feeling. I don't trust Marvelous Joe, and I don't want anybody getting hurt."

Sloane wasn't buying it—Jack obviously had some ulterior motive here—but he didn't argue.

Even though he was ostensibly Jack's superior, Sloane was never comfortable giving the man direct orders. He signed off on the mission and requisitioned the necessary funds.

And now Jack was standing at the foot of one of the most famous statues in the world, holding a suitcase and waiting for Marvelous Joe. The plaza at the base of the statue was normally off-limits to cars, but Jack had greased a couple of palms and had been able to drive right up. He parked his car in the shadows, across the plaza from where he was to meet Joe. He didn't expect any trouble—Joe was supposed to come alone, and he had never double-crossed Jack before—but, because it was his nature, Jack had taken certain precautions, including setting the meet in this particular spot.

Corcovado was located in the Tijuca Forest, the largest forest in the world completely contained in an urban area. It was a rugged, mountainous region that cut through the center of the city and provided a home to myriad species of plants and animals. It also provided Jack Bristow with a secluded place to meet with Marvelous Joe and, more importantly, a single, easily surveilled access road.

He walked to the edge of the plaza and looked

down on the thickly forested mountain below. A car was approaching. Jack could hear it well before he caught a glimpse of it rounding a corner. The car was traveling slowly, without lights, but he caught the glint of moonlight off of metal as it wound its way upward.

He closed his eyes and listened to the sound of the motor. Just before the car reached the summit, Jack picked up a slight screech of brakes engaging, accompanied by the engine downshifting. The car had paused briefly—less than a quarter mile from the top—and Jack assumed that it was dropping off passengers. It appeared that Marvelous Joe was double-crossing him after all.

Jack pulled out his gun and double-checked that it was loaded and ready to fire. He considered screwing the silencer onto the barrel but decided against it. They were isolated up here, and he preferred to use an unsilenced .45 whenever possible—the noise tended to be a great help in instilling fear and confusion. He tucked the gun into his overcoat and then melted back into the shadows at the base of the statue and waited.

The car, a beat-up sedan with a shattered rear window, pulled up and blinked its lights twice.

Marvelous Joe, snappily dressed in a head-to-toe fur coat that cost more than the car, and sporting a mouthful of gold that was new since Jack had last seen him, turned off the engine and climbed out of the driver's seat. "Hello?" he called out in a thick Portuguese accent. "Anyone there?"

Jack stepped forward, out of the shadows—suitcase in one hand, the other deep in the pocket of his overcoat. "Hello, Joe. Nice teeth."

Marvelous Joe gasped and turned pale. "Jack . . . what a surprise. I . . . I didn't expect you to come yourself."

"I hope you don't mind. I needed to get out of the office, stretch my legs a bit."

It was quite clear that Joe *did* mind—very much so—but he tried to keep up a good front. "No, I don't mind. It's good to see you, my friend." His eyes were darting around wildly, searching for his backup.

"I brought you the money." Jack held up the briefcase. "I'm assuming you have the disk?"

Joe needed to buy some time. "Actually, Jack, the disk is back at my place, in the favela," he stammered, referring to one of the crime-ridden shantytowns that dotted the hillsides of Rio. "If I had known that you were coming yourself, I would have brought it, of course. I was just being cautious. Why don't you come with me back to my place and we can make the exchange there? Have a drink, maybe?"

"I don't think so, Joe. Maybe next time." The crunch of a shoe on gravel had alerted Jack to the fact that Joe's friends had arrived. He began to back away, as if to leave, and four thugs—younger and not quite as expensively dressed as Joe—leaped from the shadows and fanned out behind their leader, doing their best to appear menacing. In the moonlight, Jack could see that all four of them were brandishing pistols. He had a powerful urge to laugh at them, but managed to keep it under control.

"There's not going to be a next time, Jack," Joe called out, cocky now that his reinforcements had arrived. He started to give his men the order to fire, but before the first word had even left his lips, two shots rang out—and two of his men dropped to the ground.

Jack threw himself to the right and rolled toward the cover of a cement trash barrel as the remaining thugs opened fire. He withdrew the pistol from his pocket, noting the smoking hole in the fabric as he did. *Ruined another overcoat,* he thought as bullets whizzed by overhead. "Kill him!" Joe shrieked. Jack only paused behind the trash barrel for a moment before making a dash for the statue's mammoth base.

As he rounded the corner of the pedestal, a shot ricocheted off the cement near his head and Jack let go of the briefcase. It fell to the ground with a clatter, but Jack didn't pause to pick it up. He ran for the low stone retaining wall on the far side of the statue and vaulted over it. He hit the ground on the other side and crouched down, completely hidden in the shadows.

He could hear Joe yelling to his comrades in Portuguese. "Forget him, we got the money. Let's go." Three car doors slammed in quick succession, the engine turned over, and the tires kicked up a spray of gravel.

Jack waited a few seconds, then climbed back over the wall and walked calmly to the far side of the plaza, where he could see the car speeding away down the mountain road. No need for stealth now—the headlights clearly marked the vehicle's progress. Jack knew that Joe would be busy jimmying the locks on the briefcase. Any second now, he was going to open that case and find it full of newspaper. If he looked any closer, he'd probably find the false bottom underneath the papers.

Jack pulled a simple, two-button detonator from his pocket. He flipped the safety to the off position and, without the least hesitation, depressed the trigger button.

The fireball rose fifty feet in the air and the explosion rang out across the forest, echoed by the cacophony raised by thousands of creatures whose sleep had been disturbed. Jack walked quickly across the plaza to where his car was parked, pausing only to retrieve another briefcase—the one that actually contained the money—from the trash barrel where he had stashed it earlier in the evening. "I'm sorry you had to see that," he said to the statue as he started the car and drove off.

The next morning dawned clear and beautiful. Jack arose early, showered and shaved, and dressed in a light-colored linen suit. It was a good deal less formal than what he would normally wear, but he needed to blend in today. He breakfasted in the hotel restaurant, then checked out and drove to the airport. He returned the rental car and then stashed his luggage in a locker—except for the briefcase full of cash. He checked in with APO and left a message for Sloane that the deal had gone south, that there was no disk, and that he would be returning to Los Angeles on a commercial flight that left at five in the evening. He hung up without elaborating and placed his phone in the locker, along with the comms that he always kept with him. He was now effectively untraceable—off the grid for an afternoon in Rio.

Jack hailed a cab and gave the driver directions that more or less took them in the opposite direction of where he wanted to go. It was probably overkill, but old habits die hard. He switched cabs twice, eyes constantly peeled for tails, before actually heading to his destination—and yet he still had the driver drop him a half mile from the actual spot.

It was warm enough for Jack to remove his jacket as he walked along the beach in Ipanema—one of the nicest, most expensive neighborhoods in the city. This beach was world renowned for the beauty of its women, and the smallness of their swimwear—and Jack found himself agreeing on both counts.

He grabbed a corner stool at the outdoor bar that had been specified in the message—a thatch-roofed, open-walled affair, right on the beach—and ordered a mai tai from the friendly bartender, who was every bit as beautiful as the girls frolicking on the beach. His drink came—icy and delicious—and Jack settled in to watch the parade of barely clad bodies passing by.

"I hear there was some nastiness up on Corcovado last night," a familiar voice piped up from behind Jack. "That wouldn't have had anything to do with you, would it, Jack?"

He didn't even turn around to answer. "No, but I have a briefcase full of the United States government's cash here—just in case you're running short of funds."

"Fortunately, my finances are well in hand. I see that you got my message. Glad to know you still read the *Times*."

Jack smiled and turned to greet Connors—the man who he was closest to in all the world—with a hug. It had been thirty years since the last time, but this ritual greeting never failed to amuse Jack. He was not by nature a hugger—but with Connors, you didn't get much choice.

"It's good to see you," Jack said when Connors pulled away. "We didn't really get a chance to catch up last time."

"Oh, yes," Connors laughed, "something about a gun battle and a fire and me fleeing down a mountain, wasn't there?"

"Something like that," Jack said. "I should have realized that you would wind up here."

"Why, Jack, whatever do you mean?" Connors said with mock innocence.

"Rio de Janeiro. That means 'River of January' in Portuguese, I believe."

"Does it? How appropriate," Connors said with a comical shrug.

He turned to order a drink—a mai tai as well—and Jack took a moment to regard his friend's appearance. The past three months had not been kind to Connors. He was as dapper as ever—the inevitable white rose on the inevitable seersucker—but he had lost a great deal of weight and his face was pale and drawn. Jack could see that the disease had advanced, and realized that this would most likely be the last time they saw each other.

Connors received his drink from the beautiful bartender—who had been thoroughly charmed by his flirting—and they took their drinks to one of a handful of small tables that were set up on the sand. Connors raised his glass to Jack in salute. "To a successful game," he intoned, and took a drink.

Shaking off his gloomy thoughts, Jack raised his glass in return, determined to enjoy the time that they *did* have left. "A little too close for comfort there at the end," he replied, "but a success. Cheers." He followed Connors's lead and took a deep drink.

"Where are Christopher and May?" Jack asked after drinking. "I was hoping to meet them."

"They have graciously allowed us this time to catch up, but will be joining us for lunch in a few hours."

Jack smiled. "I wanted to introduce myself at the clinic, but it might have been a bit awkward—considering I had your blood all over my hands. How's the arm, by the way?"

"You left a terrible scar, but then sewing was never your strong suit. I suppose I should just be grateful that you showed up when you did." Connors's laugh dissolved into a fit of coughing that both he and Jack, in unspoken agreement, chose to ignore.

When Connors had recovered a bit, Jack continued talking. "I suppose, in the long run, it was a good thing that the Leuba's hit team showed up—the attack probably sold your death better than the car crash was going to—but it's a shame about the clinic."

Connors agreed. "At least none of the patients was hurt. Christopher and May hope to open a new facility somewhere once the dust has settled. I felt terrible for them. There were so many people milling around, I wasn't able to sneak back and let them know that I'd survived for almost an entire day. You should have heard May scream when I showed up."

"I can imagine," Jack replied.

"And how is Sydney?" Connors inquired.

The very mention of his daughter's name brought a smile to Jack's face. "She's well. I think she's happy that I've 'returned to normal,'" he laughed. "I'm so glad that you finally got a chance to meet her."

"She was an absolute joy to work with—and even lovelier than you described. You're a very lucky man, Jack Bristow. We both are. I'm fairly certain that neither of us deserve such fantastic offspring."

"I will drink to that," Jack said, and did so.

"Your entire team at—what was it called again? APO? The entire group was delightful."

Jack nodded and wholeheartedly concurred. "They are good, aren't they? Marcus, Nadia, the whole group. Marshall is a piece of work, but I've never seen a tech man that comes anywhere close. I've even been making some slight effort toward warming up to Agent Vaughn—not that he deserves it."

"I rather liked him, myself. But I can see it in your eyes—no one will ever be good enough for her, will they?"

"Never," Jack agreed, "but I suppose that if she has to be with someone, there are worse choices out there. Of course, if you tell anyone that I said that, I'll deny it."

They were silent for a moment—both of them realizing that, even if he wanted to, Connors was never going to get a chance to tell anyone what Jack had said. Jack noticed that his friend was absentmindedly rubbing his bare finger. "Missing your ring?" he asked.

Connors realized what he was doing and laughed. "Every day. But I suppose our good friend patient twenty-three had more need of it than I did."

"Who was he? I didn't get a chance to ask at the clinic."

"He was a victim of my final intelligence mission—after you left."

There was no anger—no accusation—in what Connors said, but the mood at their table shifted, became a little strained. These two men had never been less than the best of friends, but there was obviously some unresolved tension revolving around their relationship. Jack seemed to be at a loss for words, so Connors continued.

"I attempted one final game after your departure: a terrorist group, based in Belgrade. I was angry—angry and arrogant, I suppose—and I wanted to prove that I could handle things without your help. It was in the back room of a big restaurant. There were civilians—waiters, a couple of prostitutes. It spiraled completely out of control. I had to go to backup protocols—blew the whole place up. It was . . . appalling. Twenty-three was a bartender at the restaurant, and the only survivor—if you can call that surviving." Connors's guilt was palpable.

Jack attempted to raise his spirits. "And you cared for him for all those years? You're a good man, Reg. I don't know anyone else who would have done that."

The smile that came to Connors's lips was as sad as it could be and still be called a smile. "Yes, after I destroyed his mind, I cared for him," he said bitterly. "I kept him with me and I cared for him—to assuage my guilt, and to be a constant reminder that what I had done was an abomination. Eventually I struck on the idea of opening the clinic and devoting myself to research of a more humane nature than that which I had practiced in the past."

"I'm sorry I wasn't there for you," Jack said, simply and sincerely.

Connors waved off the apology. "I was angry at the time—hell, I was angry for thirty years—but you were right to leave. Do you remember what you said to me, Jack? After Laura got pregnant and you decided to pack it in and concentrate on straight espionage?" Jack shook his head and Connors continued. "The last thing you said to me was 'find your family and make it up to them.' I never forgot that, but it was a long time before I realized that you knew what you were talking about."

"They do make it all worthwhile, don't they?" Jack said quietly.

'They do indeed. And *I* will drink to that." He

took a deep swallow of his drink and then tried to lighten the mood a bit. "And after thirty-some-odd years of not speaking to you, I came waltzing back into your life, begging for your help. And you didn't even hesitate."

Jack's response, and his smile, was immediate. "What are partners for?"

They sat in comfortable silence for a while, watching a group of young men on the beach, practicing the acrobatic, swirling movements of capoeira: the distinctly Brazilian sport that appeared to be half dance, half martial art. The beach was thronged with tanned, healthy people laughing and flirting and playing games as if their lives depended on it.

"So what happens now?" Jack finally asked. "Where do you go from here?"

"From here," Connors replied with a grin, "*we* go to lunch with Christopher and May. After which, I'm afraid, we'll have to put you in a cab and send you off to the airport. From there, I imagine that the three of us will stay in Rio for a while. The River of January, wasn't it? The river of beginnings and endings—seems like a good choice, somehow. Eventually—sooner rather than later, I'm afraid—

Christopher and May will move on. Found a new clinic, continue my research, and maybe—when they're sure it won't be misused—they can introduce the world to the other January. How does that sound?"

"Sounds like a plan to me," Jack responded. "What time is lunch?"

Connors checked his watch. "Soon enough," he replied, "but not so soon that we don't have time for a game."

Jack smiled, and then laughed warmly. "I hope you remember whose turn it is to start."

Connors conceded that Jack had won their last game, more than thirty years ago, and allowed him to move first. "I believe I'll play it safe today. King's pawn to E-four," Jack said, and the game was on.

They made their moves quickly and with total confidence—completely evenly matched—and both of them thought it was the most satisfying game that they had ever played.